STAGE-STRUCK
by
Jean Carew

Author of "DEBUTANTE NURSE" *and* "SWING FROM A STAR"

Kate Harmon, sixteen, saw herself as a great actress. A leading role in her high school junior play gave her a taste for the footlights and, with the help of Martina Dawson, her teacher-coach, she followed that by the organization of a summer little theatre group during vacation.

Various students rallied round, and Martina even procured the services of a professional director from New York, Peter Howard. Although Peter was not yet famous and his experience had been confined to off-Broadway, Kate saw in him the answer to all her dreams, both romantic and theatrical.

But the end of summer brought the end of dreams, and the beginning of maturity.

STAGE-STRUCK

STAGE-STRUCK

by

JEAN CAREW

Alouette Romance
By
Sharon Publications, Inc.
Closter, NJ

STAGE-STRUCK

Chapter 1

The solemn little group of five walked purposefully down the dirt road toward old Jim Reynold's farm, in the golden twilight of the perfect day, late in June. In the lead was Martina Dawson, young and attractive high school teacher who was trying in vain to keep her dark, fly-away hair in some semblance of order for this all-important interview. On either side of her, slightly behind her, were two young girls, her pupils, Kate Scott and Stella Rand. She had coached them in the junior class play of the high school, presented to an enthusiastic audience just two weeks before.

Bringing up the rear were two young men who had also been members of the junior class. Gilbert Morehouse, the taller of the two, looked as alert as a boxer about to enter the ring for a title bout. And even Henry Johnson, voted the class clown in the yearbook, looked serious. It was Gil Morehouse who broke the silence.

"You know," he said portentously, "this old Jim Reynolds is a perfect square. Chances are he'll say no before we even ask him for the use of that broken-down barn of his."

"Now, Gilbert," the teacher reproved him, "if you take that attitude you will surely be turned down. The thing to do is to put the proposition up to him as a community gesture. If you will let me do the talking perhaps I can smooth the way for the actual request."

"Miss Dawson, you've done so much for us already," Kate Scott said in her slightly husky voice, "we hate to ask you to take on the whole burden of the summer theatre idea. You've already arranged for a professional director to come from New York, and you've got the School Board to approve the loan of the stage scenery. I think there ought to be something that we should do for ourselves."

"Especially," the redhead on the other side of the teacher chimed in gloomily, "when we are almost sure to get a turndown. I know you want us to be hopeful, but there are some people, like Daddy, who don't want to give us a chance to prove we can really act."

"Maybe he thinks 'all the world's a stage'," Henry Johnson put in with a feeble attempt at levity, "and everybody's a player or something, so why should he shell out good hard cash—five hundred dollars of it—to have a guy from New York teach us how to be actors? Oh well," he sighed in mock despair, "we're just footprints on the sands of time anyway."

Kate turned and gave Henry what she felt was a withering look. But Henry, who was as susceptible to her long-lashed amber eyes as every other boy in her class, did not seem particularly dashed. "It isn't as if we were asking Stella's father to *give* us five hundred dollars," she said impatiently. "It's only a loan. Surely if we are ready to put on the show in August, and if we advertise it right, we'll make at least that much money on it, with all the summer people here. I'm sure we can repay every penny."

"You are floating on cloud nine," Gil Morehouse said sourly. "Who ever heard of a banker loaning money without collateral? As a matter of fact, who ever heard of Farmer Reynolds loaning anything at all—even an old barn?"

"Collateral!" Henry Johnson murmured dreamily. "My, what big words we know! Could be the gook has brains."

For answer Gil Morehouse pummeled his friend in the ribs and stiff-armed him over to the side of the road. Henry Johnson whirled with mock belligerence, but before he could retaliate Martina Dawson said sharply:

"Cut it out, boys. We're almost at the Reynolds' place, and I can see Jim Reynolds just coming out of the barn. You know," she said, in an attempt to be fair, "Farmer Reynolds has to work mighty hard for the money he gets. Taking care of sixteen milk cows means a lot of work, and everyone admits that he takes the finest care of his cattle. I understand this year he even has a few chickens, so I imagine he is having a rough time making ends meet. If he does refuse us, don't think too harshly of him."

"We won't exactly put a hex on him," Gil Morehouse promised. "But I'm giving it to you straight, Miss Dawson: this is the only barn near town that isn't being used. My paper route covers an area of about twenty-five miles and I know what I'm talking about."

The little group was approaching a small two-story house that was trimly painted and set back from the road behind a low picket fence. The house, indeed, seemed almost lost between two huge barns flanking it on either side. There were also a number of sheds for storing tools and farm machinery and a small one-story building set apart from them and fenced in with chicken wire, which Kate Scott rightly surmised had been set aside for the new chicks. She saw that Jim Reynolds had caught sight of them and was eying them suspiciously. His loose-jointed figure was clad in a pair of dusty overalls, and his bewhiskered face was shaded by a raggedy straw hat.

"Anybody wanna bet he spends so much time reading the shaving cream ads that he can't get around to using a razor?" Henry Johnson murmured under his breath.

"Stop yakking, Freckles," Kate commanded.

Martina Dawson stepped ahead of the group and advanced toward the picket fence with a determined smile. She caught a slight movement of

ruffled curtains at a front window and guessed
that Hallie Reynolds, Jim's wife, was keeping a
sharp eye on these unannounced visitors.

"Good day, Mr. Reynolds," Martina called
brightly, and Kate remembered how often she
had called her classes to attention with that same
note of buoyant enthusiasm. "It's such a lovely
day we thought we'd walk over to your place instead of driving. I am Martina Dawson—one of
the high school teachers. These are some of the
pupils who will be seniors next year. They have
come up with an idea, and if we could take just a
few minutes of your time—"

Jim Reynolds had been standing stock-still,
but as they neared the gate in the fence apparently he decided that he had better head them off
before they got into the yard. He shambled toward them and, without acknowledging the in-
troduction, said laconically:

"Weather-breeder, that's what it is. Shouldn't
wonder if we get a smackin' thunderstorm 'fore
morning. Gonna flatten down all the hay in the
south meadow." He had reached the gate and
put two calloused hands on top of it as if the
teacher had tried to break in.

"I'm sorry to hear that," Miss Dawson said sympathetically, and Kate noticed that her voice quavered slightly in spite of her effort to appear at ease. "But that isn't what we came to talk to you about, really—the weather, I mean."

"If it's some new school assessment," Jim Reynolds said belligerently, "I ain't contributin' nothin'. Hallie and me never had no kids, and yet we're payin' through the nose for that new-fangled schoolhouse they built five years ago. People who has a raft of children oughta support 'em, I say, or put 'em to work, not ask the neighbors to work their fingers to the bone."

"But, Mr. Reynolds," Kate Scott could not help interrupting, "that isn't what we came to talk about at all. Miss Dawson is not acting for the School Board. She is only acting as our friend and giving us advice."

"Oh, what's the use?" Stella Rand said with irritation. Her red curls seemed to glow more brightly at the farmer's ungracious attitude. "I doubt very much if Mr. Reynolds cares to hear what we have to say, unless it has something to do with cows."

"You're the banker's daughter, ain't you?"

Reynolds demanded. "You look some like him, and seems as though you got his temper, too."

"What we came for was to inquire about that barn across the road," Martina Dawson said hastily, nodding toward the structure in back of them. "I understand your property extends on both sides of the road, and I take it that barn belongs to you. Is that right?"

"What if it does?" the farmer asked, bristling.

"Just that you don't use it much during the summer," Gil Morehouse put in. "I figure you use it mainly to store surplus hay over the winter."

"Seems to me you're mighty interested in other folks' business," said Jim Reynolds grimly. "The way you come roarin' past the house here in that rattletrap junk heap of yours, bellowin' at the top of your lungs, is enough to make the milk turn sour. Just mind your own business like I mind mine."

"So much for the golden-voiced baritone," Henry Johnson muttered. "I guess that'll learn you, young fella, to keep your big trap shut. I can just see the headlines now: 'Promising young singer has reputation for souring cows' milk.' My lad, your success is assured." He shrank back as Gilbert made a threatening gesture.

Martina Dawson quelled the boys with a glance and then turned back to the farmer. Kate saw her chin lift and her eyes flash as she prepared to do battle for the home of the new summer theatre.

"Mr. Reynolds, I want to make this perfectly clear at the start," she began. "We are not asking for the loan of your barn for ourselves alone. It will really be a community project."

She now had Jim Reynolds' fascinated attention. He had started to turn back toward the barn, signifying that the interview was over, but he immediately faced about and gave the teacher a suspicious look.

"You want to borrow my barn?" he asked incredulously. "What for? I won't have no riding horses in there, and I won't tolerate any such going's-on. This ain't no dude ranch."

"But that isn't it at all," Kate was moved to protest. "We're forming a summer theatre group, Mr. Reynolds, and we're going to put on a play that will bring people to the community from miles around; especially summer visitors."

"Yes, and we're going to have a professional director work with us," Stella Rand added. "My father is paying for him to come and coach us."

"Yeah," Henry Johnson muttered, "we're going to put little old Squaresville right on the map."

Farmer Reynolds was shaking his head in a decided negative. But he had only one word to say, and he said it with decision: "Nope."

"You haven't even thought about it," Gil Morehouse accused the loose-jointed man behind the picket fence. The farmer's shambling figure suddenly seemed to have been reinforced with steel. "Besides, it won't be any trouble to you. The barn is across the road, and the summer people who come to the show won't trouble you at all. We'll do all the building, put up a stage at one end, make a sign to hang out over the door. "We'll call it," he said with sudden inspiration " 'Reynolds' Summer Theatre.' "

"Nope."

"Before you turn us down completely," Martina Dawson said with a last despairing resolve to obtain the barn, "think of what this will mean to the young people of Clyde's Gap. Some of them will undoubtedly be professionals one day, and I am sure they will never forget the man who gave them their first chance. Also, you will have the satisfaction of knowing that, although you have no children of your own, you have made a great contribution to those of the next generation. Please do say we can borrow the barn for just these few weeks. We plan to present the play in August, and it will run for about three weeks. By the first of September you will have the barn back again all to yourself, and I guarantee it will be exactly as we found it."

"Nope. Get some other dumb fool to loan you his barn. I don't owe anything to Clyde's Gap. Can't even sell my milk to the local store; I gotta drag it twenty-five miles over to the pasteurizing plant and drive twenty-five miles back. When you count the cost of gas and oil and the wear and tear on the car, there ain't no profit in it. All I ever got out of Clyde's Gap," the farmer added bitterly, "was a raise in taxes. Like I said, you go peddle your apples somewhere else."

"There's no other barn around here that isn't

being used," Gil Morehouse burst out without thinking. "I travel this route every week day, and believe me, if there had been any other place, we would not have bothered you."

For the first time Jim Reynolds seemed to be enjoying himself. He looked around at the earnest faces of the teacher and the young students around her, and something that was almost a smile creased his lined face.

"Now ain't that just too bad!" he said sarcastically. "You not only gotta have a barn to do your play-actin'; you gotta have *my* barn. Well, I said it before and I'll say it again. The answer is—"

"Nope," said Henry Johnson, in such a perfect imitation of the farmer's truculent tone that Stella could not repress a giggle.

It did not matter now, Kate thought dully. Apparently there was no argument that would appeal to this stubborn old man. She saw her bright dream of a summer theatre and the chance to try out their talents in a glamorous profession completely dissipated. Martina Dawson had once suggested that they use the Town Hall to put on the play, but to Kate this would have been a total loss. Traditionally a summer theatre was housed in a local barn; there was an atmosphere and a charm about the rustic setting that added to the attraction of the play even when the group was professional. Amateur actors certainly needed all the atmosphere they could get.

Kate's eyes looked past the farmer toward the cluster of buildings in the back of the house and toward the chicken house with its fenced-in yard. Since there was no hope that Farmer Reynolds would change his mind, she said critically:

"Why aren't your chicks out in the yard? I should think they would be better off running around outside than cooped up in that hot old brooder house."

"I ain't heard tell that you and your Maw ever raised a chicken in your lives," Farmer Reynolds drawled. "You can't come around here and tell me how to run my business. That's one of the reasons you can't have my barn," he said to Martina Dawson. "Give the young 'uns an inch these days and they'll take a mile. First thing you know they'll want me to get a milk storage tank; never mind that it would cost three thousand dollars. For your information, Miss Knowitall, them's chicks ain't completely feathered out. When they are, they'll get plenty of fresh air."

But Kate refused to be slapped down. If the old farmer insisted upon being disagreeable, she would be too. "I still say those chicks would be better off outdoors," she repeated. "I bet they're practically gasping for air right now. You must have a powerful heater in there, the way smoke is pouring out of the houses.

Kate was unprepared for the instant reaction her words received. Farmer Reynolds spun around and looked toward the brooder house in consternation. He stood as if paralyzed; smoke was indeed pouring out through every crack and crevice of the small building.

"Hey, the place is on fire!" Gil Morehouse shouted. "Come on, Henry; we've got to get those chicks out of there." He vaulted over the picket fence as he spoke, and Henry followed him. Before the farmer had recovered from his stupefaction, the boys had reached the brooder house and were about to go in when Hallie Reynolds burst out of the kitchen door.

"The brooder house is on fire!" she yelled

shrilly and unnecessarily. "Here's a coupla cartons, boys. See if you can save any of the chicks." She threw two boxes at them as she spoke, and Henry scooped one up and dashed inside after Gil. "By the time *you* get moving," Hallie Reynolds muttered to her husband, "you'll lose the whole flock."

Kate and Stella burst through the gate and ran toward the brooder house. Martina Dawson put a restraining hand on each of them as they started to go by her.

"Let the boys handle this," she admonished. "You would only be in the way. We'll go into the house and phone the fire department."

"Some good that will do," Stella commented. "Before they get out here the chicks will be burned to a cinder." But nevertheless she followed Kate and Martina into the spotless kitchen where the phone was located.

It did seem hopeless, Kate thought, as the teacher spun the dial. Not only had they failed in their mission to obtain the use of the barn, but they had been witnesses to what was for a small farmer a tragic loss. Moreover, she was sure that by some obscure line of reasoning, the farmer would blame them for keeping him occupied when he might have prevented the fire if he had been free to continue his accustomed routine and perhaps check on the brooder house in time.

Chapter 2

Evangeline Scott regarded her daughter fondly. She was a small, spare woman, angular where Kate was softly rounded, but with the same amber eyes and the same ash-blonde hair, now streaked with gray. Even while she listened to Kate's excited account of the afternoon's interview with Farmer Reynold's, Mrs. Scott's fingers never stopped their busy task of hemming one of her neighbor's dresses. The small pension she had received since her husband died was not quite adequate, but with the supplemental sewing she was able to do they lived quite comfortably.

The widow was intensely proud of Kate's debut in the junior class play and had thought her heart would burst at the prolonged applause her daughter had received when the curtain fell. She was enthusiastic, too, about Kate's idea for a summer theatre group. But Evangeline Scott was well aware that there might be pitfalls in the way of a young amateur breaking into the professional theatre. She did not want her Kate to be hurt.

"I don't wonder Jim Reynolds refused you the use of his barn," she said as Kate described the farmer's reluctance—in fact, his absolute refusal—to loan the barn even for a few weeks. "Even in school he had a reputation for refusing to loan so much as a pencil to any of his classmates. And I'm sure he's never seen a play or even a movie in his entire lifetime."

"But, Mom, wait'll you hear," Kate said gaily, her golden eyes sparkling with mischief. "You wouldn't believe what happened after that. Now don't interrupt me; I want to tell you exactly how it was."

Kate went on to detail the many arguments the little group had advanced in order to get the barn, and the cool way their ideas had been received by Farmer Reynolds. Evangeline Scott nodded as she continued her fine sewing. Then

Kate, eager that her mother should have the entire picture, repeated the remark she had made to Jim Reynolds about letting the chicks out in the yard and his cutting jibe about her knowledge of chickens.

"He needn't be so uppity," Mrs. Scott said sharply, forgetting that she was not to interrupt. "As a matter of fact, your father and I had fifty chicks when you were about five years old, and you often helped me to feed them and to gather the eggs. But Jim was right, of course," she conceded grudgingly. "They should not be let out until they're fully feathered."

Kate did not bother to reply to this. She rushed on to relate how the fire had started and how Gil and Henry had dashed into the burning house and had rescued almost all the chicks. They were huddled in a corner, cheeping pitifully, and both boys scooped them into the boxes and passed them outside to Jim Reynolds. Jim's wife, meanwhile, kept up a nagging commentary on the subject of kerosene brooders in general and the secondhand one Jim had bought in particular. Miss Dawson, Stella and Kate could only stand by helplessly and wait for the fire engine.

When it came at last, the brooder house was only a smoking ruins. They played the hoses on it while Jim Reynolds carried the chickens to one of the big barns.

Since there was nothing else they could do, Miss Dawson had led her pupils toward the road, and they had reached the picket fence before Jim Reynolds came out of the barn and shouted for them to come back. He thanked the boys for saving the chicks and even acknowledged that if Kate had not been there, the fire might have gone unnoticed until it was too late.

" 'Figure I owe you young 'uns somethin',' " Kate repeated, describing the farmer's sheepish expression. " 'I guess if you want to use the barn, it's all right with me. But first off you gotta paint it outside. I got the paint, but I'm so dog-goned busy I don't know when I'll get around to it.' For a minute I thought Miss Dawson was going to faint." Kate laughed. "Then we accepted his offer so fast it wasn't even funny, and we practically ran down the road before he could change his mind."

Evangeline Scott, who had paused in her sewing to hear the details of the fire, again resumed her work, smiling as if to herself.

"This will surely be a red-letter day in the history of Clyde's Gap," she said happily. "The first time Jim Reynolds has ever been known to make a generous gesture! Of course he is getting his barn painted, and that will take your new stage company some time."

"Oh, no, Mom," Kate cried, dancing around the room in sheer exuberance. "Henry says he can get permission to use a spray gun for paint from his father's stock in the hardware store. In fact, he is going to borrow two guns, and they figure they can do the job in less than a day. It's the inside of the barn that worries us," she went on, frowning. "The floor is pretty uneven, and we'll have to smooth it out a bit. Then there's the stage to be built and the electric wire to be strung. Of course there is one outlet in the barn already, but we need several more. The boys can do the actual work, but we'll have to get the town electrician to check it over before we turn on the juice."

Evangeline Scott laid down her sewing and got up from the chair. "You'll find there's a lot to do before you can even start rehearsals," she warned. "But in the meantime I think we'd both better have some supper, or else the leading lady," her indulgent smile softened the words, "will be famished."

Not only Kate and her "company" were busy in the days that followed; in addition; ten other high school classmates were drafted to help build the stage, smooth down the floor of the barn, remove the odds and ends of equipment that Farmer Reynolds had stored there, hang curtains to form dressing rooms and transport the scenery from the high school basement. One of the talented girls was given the task of lettering the sign that would hang above the double door. Gil Morehouse insisted that it read: "Reynold's Summer Theatre," because he had promised that this would be the name. Martina Dawson was everywhere, advising and helping to prepare the theatre.

One day she came over to where Kate and Stellla Rand were busy wiping off the "flats"— the canvas sections that would form the background for the new play.

"I've just heard from Peter Howard, Stella,"

she said worriedly, "and he has another offer to direct a series of plays at a summer theatre in Maine. I know you are convinced that your father will advance us the five hundred dollars we have promised to pay him, but I am reluctant to ask Peter to give us this opportunity unless I can send him a check in advance. We are really very fortunate to be able to get Peter Howard up here at any price. He is considered one of the most promising talents in the Broadway theatre, and a few years from now he will be getting a fabulous salary. He is worth it," she added loyally. "I studied dramatics for a year at the University, and Peter was the most brilliant student they ever had."

Stella Rand got slowly to her feet. Her mop of curly red hair was wind-blown and she had a long smudge across one cheek. But Kate thought as she looked at her that Stella had never seemed more alive. Her expression, however, was marred by a look of discontent.

"Miss Dawson, I've been trying to persuade Dad to help us out. I have told him it was only a temporary loan and that he would get back every penny of it. But he insists upon regarding the whole thing as a big joke, and even Mother hasn't been able to make him take us seriously. When I talk about going on the stage," she added, "Dad just says: 'that'll be the day.' But I'll try again," she said with resignation.

"Maybe if I came along with you," Kate offered, "we could really convince him that we mean to make a success of this project."

"Oh, would you!" For the first time Kate saw her classmate unsure of herself. Usually Stella had a redheaded arrogance that brooked no interference or advice. But apparently tackling her father on a matter of some importance was something else again. Stella glanced at her wrist watch and turned to the teacher.

"Miss Dawson, if we leave right now, I can catch Dad before he gets away from the bank. I've been touching up this piece of scenery, and I hate to leave it lying here. . . ."

Martina Dawson assured the girls that she would see to it that the scenery was placed under cover and that the curtains Kate was so busily hemming would be folded and put away for the next day's work. By common consent the girls got into Stella's small compact car—a present from her father for successfully completing her junior year.

"Must you go quite so fast?" Kate protested as they took the double S turns leading into the village of Clyde's Gap with no slowing down of pace.

"I like to go fast," Stella said, cutting in front of a truck just in time to miss a car in the opposite lane. "Dad would be furious if he knew, but I've had this little bug up to eighty. Don't bother about my speed, Kate. Concentrate on how we're going to win over Dad."

Kate did concentrate and realized that they faced a formidable task. Stella's father was a big, well-fed, balding bear of a man whose genial hail-fellow-well-met manner was belied by the shrewdness of his gaze. Kate had never seen him when he was not smiling and jovial, but she had an uneasy suspicion that Mr. Rand could be stern upon occasion. Stella confirmed this as she brought the car to a stop and both girls ran toward the three-story granite building that housed the bank of Clyde's Gap.

"Dad will be as cross as a hornet," Stella said apprehensively. "He doesn't like me to bother him at the bank. But he's attending a bankers' meeting tonight over in Middleboro, and Miss Dawson must have an answer today. Keep your fingers crossed, Kate."

The guard was about to lock up the doors, but recognized Stella and let her slide through with Kate before he put on the padlock. The tellers and clerks were still busy at their desks, and in a railed-off enclosure John Rand sat with dignity behind a huge mahogany desk. A small, nervous-looking man sat facing him and was apparently the only customer left. Kate's heart sank as she saw that the banker was obviously annoyed that his visitor had overstayed banking hours. He did not appear to notice his daughter and her friend come in, but Kate was sure he was well aware of their presence.

The conversation went on for a few minutes more, and then abruptly the banker got to his feet. With some reluctance the little man rose, too, and stood meekly twisting his cap in his hands.

"My decision is final," the banker boomed. "You won't show enough margin of profit on that new venture to interest us here at the bank. I am afraid we can't loan you any amount at all. Good day to you, sir."

The little man was let out of the bank by the guard, and Stella looked toward her father expectantly. But he had settled back at his desk and was giving all his attention to the papers spread before him.

"Just our luck," Stella whispered. "Dad's in a foul mood. I'm depending on you, Kate, to come up with the right answers."

Stella's father kept them waiting a good ten minutes, and Kate was sure that he was deliberately making them uneasy. But his daughter had inherited her mother's temper as well as her red hair and became impatient at the delay. With a smothered exclamation she jumped to her feet and approached the railing. Kate followed a few paces behind.

"Dad, quit stalling." Kate thought Stella sounded just like her mother, addressing a fund raising group that had not been too successful. "Kate and I haven't got all day to hang around here, and we've got to have an answer right away."

The banker looked up with a grim expression,

and for a moment Kate was afraid he was going to order them out of the bank summarily. He did say:

"I thought I told you not to bother me here in the bank." Then his face softened. "But since you're here—"

Stella did not wait, but opened the gate in the railing and planted a firm kiss on her father's bald spot. Then, pushing aside the papers in front of him, she perched on his desk, her white shorts revealing an expanse of tanned thigh. An Italian striped jersey, shapeless and purposely a size too big, could not quite hide the youthful lines of her figure. Kate was acutely aware that her own stretched pants and red pullover were not exactly a costume appropriate for a conservative bank. But Stella seemed blithely unaware of their casual garb.

"Dad, we're in the most awful spot. You know Miss Dawson has asked this super-colossal director from Broadway, New York, to come and coach our play this summer. She knows him, Dad—they went to the University at the same time—and I don't think he would come up here if it weren't for her. And if he doesn't come, Dad I'll die—I really will die."

"I gather," her father said dryly, "that this is a question of money."

"But of course, Dad! I told you and you practically promised—"

"How much?" demanded Banker Rand, rescuing a sheaf of papers that was about to fall to the floor. "You must realize, Stella, and you too, Kate, that a man who is earning a living doesn't have much time to concentrate on theatrical problems. Even bankers," he warned, "are not made of money, you know. We must protect our investments. I repeat—how much does this Broadway character want?"

"Five hundred dollars," Stellar blurted out.

Seeing the banker's hostile expression, Kate said hurriedly:

"Peter Howard, the theatrical coach from Broadway, has been offered a job with a professional group up in Maine. But he did promise Miss Dawson that he would come here, and if we can pay him in advance I am sure he won't have anything to do with the crowd in Maine."

"I didn't approve of this summer theatre idea in the first place," Stella's father said, still scowling. "The more I hear of it the less I like it. Stella has a chance to go to a big hotel on the Cape with her mother and have a real vacation. But no, she has to hang around here. I don't see any reason why I should finance this deal, even though her mother has talked me into letting Stella go through with it."

"But, Dad, it's experience!" Stella wailed. "If I'm ever going to be on the stage—"

"Which I doubt," her father said sharply.

"Oh, Dad, don't be such a goon. Don't start chewing me out at this late date. Everything's all set."

"If everything's all set," the banker said, rising to indicate that the interview was over, "I don't see why you come around and interrupt my work. You know I have an important dinner engagement tonight, and I've got to go home and get dressed. Now run along, both of you."

"Not before you give me a check for five hundred dollars," said Stella, continuing to perch on the desk. Kate noticed that her face suddenly took on her father's stubborn look.

"Well, you won't get any five hundred dollars from me," her father said flatly. "I know better than to start handing out money. The next thing that will happen is that you will come in here and ask for another check to cover costumes—or decorations or the rent of Town Hall. . . ."

"Town Hall!" Kate echoed. "But we're not putting on the play in Town Hall. We're putting it on in a barn like other summer theatre groups do. Mr. Reynolds has said we could use his barn for as long as we need it."

"And how much is the old penny-pincher charging you?" the banker demanded. "I know Jim Reynolds, and he never gave anybody the time of day."

"He isn't charging us anything at all," Kate said quickly, "because—" She broke off as Stella pinched her arm until it hurt.

"Because he believes in our summer theatre group and he's really a very public-spirited citizen, Dad."

The banker looked from his daughter to Kate and was apparently convinced of their sincerity. "I still think Jim Reynolds must have an axe to grind. I've known him for thirty years, and this is the first time I ever heard of him giving anything away."

The banker's voice and manner were as hard as ever, but Kate noticed that he was pulling open a drawer of his desk. A second later he took out his personal checkbook and reached for his pen. Kate gave a sigh of relief. They had won! She looked at Stella who, all smiles, winked at her broadly.

"There!" he said, as he signed his name with a flourish, "let Jim Reynolds match that! Public-spirited—huh!"

Chapter 3

During the next two weeks there were a couple of disturbing incidents that made Kate wonder if she had done right in promoting the idea of the summer theatre. The events themselves were not particularly upsetting at the time, and Kate scolded herself more than once for reading important meanings into such casual happenings.

As Martina Dawson had predicted, once she telegraphed Peter Howard that the check was ready and waiting for him, he immediately telegraphed back that he would drive up from New York on the following Monday. Miss Dawson had at once called a "business meeting" of the summer theatre group, to discuss where Mr. Howard could be put up. She revealed that Mrs. Davis, proprietor of the boarding house where some of the teachers stayed, had offered to give room and board to the director at half-price as her contribution to the summer theatre movement.

"I think that is very nice of her," the teacher concluded, "because it means that we as a group can cover our director's living expenses. I am sure all of you will be willing to contribute a small portion of your allowances in order to see that our coach is comfortable and is not out of pocket for his generosity in giving us so much time."

The vote was unanimous. Each of them agreed to contribute toward what Kate labeled "the coach's fund." They were all delighted that they would not have to ask for another check from Stella's father or from any of the other townsfolk. In fact, Kate thought afterward, by this simple gesture Martina Dawson had succeeded in making them feel that they were a unified group and were operating on an almost professional level.

The following Monday, although the new coach was due to arrive, Kate temporarily forgot all about it. The vintage car, which was all they could afford, had developed a flat tire before she started out from home. She had intended to stop at the garage anyway, in order to get gas, but by the time she had wrestled the spare tire into place she was feeling cross and resentful. Kate was seldom envious, but at the moment she would have given her eyeteeth to have the new compact car that Stella Rand took as a matter of course.

It was in this frame of mind that she drove down to the garage. Her resentment was further hightened by the fact that the garage man appeared to be busy with a young man in a green convertible. He was gesturing with both hands, apparently giving directions for reaching a certain road.

"Just too bad he can't afford a road map," Kate muttered to herself. "He drives a three-thousand-dollar convertible and can't even find his way around." She decided to get the gas first, before she asked to have her tire fixed, but in her annoyance she pulled too far ahead, so that her gas tank was out of reach of the hose. Kate slammed the car into reverse and backed slowly toward the pump, her eye intent on getting the cheapest possible brand. There was a sudden grating sound, and for a second Kate could not think what it was. Then, with a sickening realization that she had hit the convertible, she stepped hard on the brake. She looked over to her right, and sure enough, the bright green paint on one side was marred by a long black scratch. The young man in the driver's seat craned his neck to look at the damage and regarded Kate coldly.

"I'm so sorry," Kate said contritely. "I was trying to get closer to this middle pump, and I didn't notice your car. . . ."

"Well, naturally," the young man said with heavy sarcasm, "you wouldn't expect to see a car stopped at a gas station."

Kate colored, knowing she was in the wrong, but perversely acting as if the driver of the convertible were at fault to some extent. If he were just asking directions there was no reason he should pull so close to the gas pumps. But it would never do, she felt, to point out that fact. He was a thin-faced young man with crew-cut dark hair and a voice that, even in her perturbation, Kate noticed was exceptionally well modulated and resonant. She said as meekly as possible:

"It's only a scratch. I will notify my insurance

company if you like, but I think Charlie here can
fix it up for you right now and send the bill to
me."

"Yes, you didn't do much damage," the young
man agreed unexpectedly. "But if you like I'll
stick around and you can try for a real smash-
eroo."

Kate lifted her chin and maintained a haughty
silence. Everything seemed to be going wrong
this morning. First there had been the car, and
now this minor accident. Kate prided herself on
her clean driving record. At the same time she
felt that the scratch on the side of the convertible
was of so little importance that only an arrogant
boor like this young man would be deliberately
rude, even insulting, about it. At the moment he
seemed to have forgotten her presence. He had
turned back to Charlie and was saying:

"I am sorry to bother you again but I am un-
familiar with this part of the country, and I wonder if I could impose on you to repeat your
directions."

"No trouble at all," Charlie said obligingly.
"But you won't need them, now that Kate Scott
is here. She's probably heading toward the Rey-

nolds farm as soon as she gets gassed up. Ain't that where you're headed, Kate?"

The young man had again fastened his intent gaze upon her, but Kate looked only at Charlie.

"If I can trouble you to put some gas in my tank," she said waspishly, "I'll leave a flat tire here and pick it up this afternoon on my way home. But I wish you'd hurry, Charlie. I was due up at the barn an hour ago."

Charlie darted around to the gas pump with alacrity, and the thin-faced young man asked quietly:

"Is this the barn where the summer theatre group is going to put on a play?"

Kate was pleasantly surprised. Evidently the news of their venture had already been noised abroad and even perfect strangers had heard of the summer theatre. Kate's thoughts broke off and she had a sudden sinking sensation in the pit of her stomach. How stupid can you be? she asked herself. There was only one person outside Clyde's Gap who knew of the summer theatre movement.

"Who are you?" she demanded.

"My name is Howard," the young man said,

confirming her fears. "I have promised to coach the play the youngsters are putting on."

Again Kate felt her resentment rising, but she fought against letting it show. It was a poor way to start with the man who might be responsible for her future success on the stage. Charlie had taken the damaged tire out of the trunk, and Kate, determinedly cheerful, called out, "Follow me!" and swung onto the highway. Peter Howard sent the convertible purring after her, and less than ten minutes later they pulled up beside the barn, now sporting its new sign, "Reynolds' Summer Theatre." The young man stopped the convertible and leaped out. He was tall as well as thin, and his frame seemed to be strung together with wires, so that every movement was abrupt and jerky. But a second later Martina Dawson came running out of the barn, her eyes sparkling with pleasure.

"Peter darling, you made it!"

"Yes, I made it," the young man said tonelessly. "But you sure gilded the lily, Tina. Why didn't you tell me that this place is at the far end of nowhere? You made it sound like a great adventure—something as daring and experimental as the theatre-in-the-round. This isn't even a *big* barn. I doubt if it will hold more than a hundred people without getting into trouble with the fire department."

"It will hold a hundred and twenty-five," Kate volunteered. "I've already checked that." The teacher had a spot of color on either cheek and seemed so angry that she could not find a ready retort.

"So you'll have a hundred twenty-five people watching my play," Peter Howard said bitterly. "How can I get a decent audience reaction, especially when I've only got a lot of amateur kids to work with?"

It was Kate's turn to wax angry. "That's the second time you've made a crack like that." she said severely. "I'll have you know, Mr. Howard, that we are all high school seniors. We are not youngsters or kids."

Martina Dawson looked at Kate as if she only then realized that the girl was present. The teacher nodded toward Stella Rand, who was standing with a dripping paintbrush, gazing open-mouthed at the new arrival. Taking the hint, Kate went over and joined Stella but could not resist a backward glance. Miss Dawson and Peter Howard were continuing their argument although, grudgingly, the coach followed Martina into the barn to inspect the facilities. When they came out a few minutes later the teacher climbed into the convertible and they sped away toward the village.

"Our new coach seems to be in quite a swizzle," Stella commented. "Do you think, Miss Dawson can persuade him to stay?"

Kate shrugged. "At this point I don't care," she said flatly. "Of all the opinionated, rude, unmannerly guys in the world he is the most. In my book he's crazy or something."

It was that very afternoon that Gil Morehouse drove up in his jalopy that signaled its coming from a quarter of a mile away. In order to leave no doubt that it was *his* car and *he* was in it, Gil was singing at the top of his voice, "Santa Lucia." The composer, however, would never have recognized the rhythm; Gil was swinging the tune in an off-beat way that gave it an entirely new tempo.

"That Gil can sure swing it," Stella remarked

as she straightened from painting the canvas flat in front of her. "Privately, I think my back is broken and I move we stop painting this antique scenery until we hear further from Mr. Peter S. Howard."

"You've got something there," Kate agreed. Her own back was aching and she had decided to call it a day. With a final shouted "Lucia," Gil Morehouse drove into the barnyard. Henry Johnson and two of his classmates came out of the barn simultaneously, carrying the tools that had been loaned them by Henry's father. But Gil was not alone. The other door of the car opened and a taller young man stepped out. His resemblance to Gil was striking, but where the newcomer was curly-haired and smiling, Gil was serious and lank-haired. Where Gil's eyes were somber and intent, the other's eyes danced as if at a secret joke.

Kate realized with a shock that this was Gil's brother Bob. He was older than most of the crowd by a couple of years; when she had been a freshman in high school, Bob Morehouse was already in his junior year. Then something had happened. Kate could not quite remember what it was, but she had gained the impression that there had been some Hallowe'en prank for which the high school principal had blamed Bob, though others had been involved. He had been suspended from school and his father had sent him away to stay with an uncle. It was slightly embarrassing to Kate to figure out what she could say to this stranger who was somehow familiar. Finally she compromised on:

"Hi, Bob!"

Henry and the other two echoed the greeting: "Hi, Bob!" Only Stella Rand did not chime in with the others. Kate glanced at her in surprise and saw that her friend was staring at Bob Morehouse as if he were a creature from outer space. Then all at once she moved forward and held out her hand.

"Hello, Bob," she said in a honeyed tone that managed to be strangely intimate. "I'm glad to see you back. Do you remember me?"

"Me forget a beautiful redheaded doll?" Bob Morehouse demanded. "You are Stella. Stella means star. You are the star of my life from now on."

"Dig the fast worker," Henry Johnson said,

breaking an awkward pause. "Maybe he'll be able to muzzle that loud-mouthed brother of his. I can see what Farmer Reynolds means when he talks about his cows giving sour milk when Gil drives by. But hey, you guys, make with the speed. Toss that saw and hammer into the back of the truck and we'll head for the store. Dad'll be breaking out in a rash if we don't show up pronto."

"Old Man Reynolds was the one who sent for Bob," Gil said proudly. "Seems he's got a broken-down tractor, and Charlie, at the garage, wanted an arm and a leg to repair it. When Reynolds heard Bob was home he got on the phone, but quick."

"Can you fix things like tractors?" Stella asked naïvely. Kate looked at her friend in astonishment. She had never known Stella to speak so sweetly or to ask such foolish questions. Even before he left Clyde's Gap Bob had been known for his mechanical skill with any type of machine.

"He's a genius," Gil said simply. "We might as well admit it. And, boy, wait'll you see that hot rod he souped up himself! That heap can really go places."

"I love to go places," Stella said demurely. "And I like to go *fast*. Will you take me for a ride in your hot rod sometime, Bob?"

"Surest thing you know, my little star," Bob said, stepping close and tweaking one of her red curls. "If I had my way it would be right now, but I promised this old duck across the way that I'd give him a hand. I'll live in hope, Baby. Don't forget to leave a candle burning in the window." He blew Stella a kiss and started across the road toward the Reynolds' cottage. His jaunty step and the tuneless whistle that floated back as he departed contrasted oddly with Kate's idea of a penitent's return.

Gil went into the barn to check on the progress of the day's work. Miss Dawson had assigned him the task of checking each night on the work that had been done. She knew that Gil's quick eyes could estimate at a glance whether the boys had been on the job or simply fooling around. Left alone with Stella, Kate looked at her friend curiously. Stella's eyes were unusually bright and her mouth looked soft and tremulous.

"I hope you're not getting ideas about Bob Morehouse," Kate warned. "You know he left

Clyde's Gap under a cloud, and I'm sure your father wouldn't like you riding around in his hot rod."

"So what?" Stella retorted airily. "I'm doing it just for kicks, and what Dad doesn't know won't hurt him."

"In other words, mind my own business," Kate said as she turned away. "Once a Girl Scout, always a Girl Scout, I guess. Always trying to do a good deed. But I'd as soon drive a car without headlights as have Bob Morehouse show off what his hot rod can do."

"You're chicken, Kate. I'll go with Bob whenever he asks me. I get a real charge out of that big boy."

Chapter 4

"This blonde girl—" began Peter Howard when he and Martina Dawson were waiting for their spaghetti with white clam sauce which was a specialty of The Bear Inn, where they were discussing the plans for the play over dinner that first night. "Are there bears around here?" he broke off to ask interestedly.

"Not since the Pilgrims landed," said Martina.

"Pity," said Peter Howard. "That blonde girl—"

"Kate Scott," Martina interrupted.

"Kate Scott," repeated Peter. "A good hug from a bear might get her over the idea she's boss of this show."

"Kate's a fine girl," Martina protested. "This show was her idea, and she got the group together. She wants to be a career actress."

"Sees herself in Hollywood, I suppose, or on television."

"I think she's aiming at the Broadway stage," said Martina.

"Any qualifications—besides her upstage manner?"

"You've got her wrong. I figured she'd be the star of this play."

"*My* play?" Peter looked stunned at the very thought.

"I wrote this play, Marty. I'm kind of sold on it. I brought along several mimeographed copies, and I'll give you a copy to mull over tonight. It doesn't take long to read it. I hope you'll like it," Peter finished. Martina was surprised at his unexpected humility. She looked at him to see if he was serious.

He was. The narrow gray eyes looked almost pleading as he returned Martina's stare.

"I'm sure it's a wonderful play," she told him. "I remember when your plays were read aloud in class, back in college, I used to be simply fascinated by their marvelous dialogue. I couldn't write worth a plugged nickel." She laughed without embarrassment. "That's why I decided that teaching was the career for me."

"It seems to agree with you, anyway," said Peter. "You're even prettier than I remembered."

"I'm surprised you remembered me at all," said Martina flippantly. "What I remember is that you never asked me for a date in those days. It burned me up, because I did want to be seen with the top man in the class."

"I was studying hard," Peter explained. "I was so wrapped up in my work that I honestly hardly knew there were any girls in the class. I lived for my playwriting, and I'm afraid I was deaf, dumb and blind to everything else."

"I'm afraid I wasn't quite so single-minded," sighed Martina. "That's probably why you're making a name for yourself in the theatrical world, while I have to settle for teaching high school students. But I still have a thing for the theatre. That's why I helped Kate Scott when she suggested this summer theatre project for Clyde's Gap. She was in the junior play, which I coached and she seemed so avid for a stage career that I thought I ought to help her all I could toward getting a start."

"This is the first play I have some hope of getting into actual production," said Peter. "I've done some directing, mostly off-Broadway plays, anything that came my way. But if I make the New York scene with this play, if it clicks—" His voice faded; then he went on: "I jumped at this chance to try it out with this high school group of yours. But somehow, I thought of them as more mature. A bunch like this is as apt to murder my play as anything else."

"Not if it's a good play," protested Martina. "They're all young, of course. But that has its advantages, too. They are serious about this project of theirs, and I think you will find they'll react in a way that will give you a fresh slant on your own work. And some of them have genuine talent."

"Name one," said Peter dismally.

"Kate Scott. I told you."

"That conceited young—"

"Wait till you get to know her. She has poise, charm and beauty. You'll fall in love with her, most likely."

"Now look here, Marty—"

"And she'll be perfect as the star of your show," Martina added, unperturbed.

"Martina Dawson will be the star."

"But I hadn't planned to be in the play myself. I'm just a sort of overseer."

"You haven't read the play yet," Peter reminded her. "The star part is definitely for you, as you will see. How I could write such a perfect vehicle when I didn't have the foggiest idea that I would be in touch with you at all—"

Martina was shaking her head vigorously.

"Perfect for you," Peter repeated. "A young woman of your appearance, manner and age is exactly what the play calls for."

"You're only clinging to me because those teen-agers have scared you," laughed Martina. But her color had risen.

"You're being silly. I see you as the star, and the rest of the cast I'll decide upon when I have my prospective troupe read lines tomorrow. Let's have a salad now, shall we?" They had finished their spaghetti and the waitress was approaching.

"How about fresh raw spinach with a vinegar dressing?"

Martina had thought of a tomato and lettuce salad with mayonnaise, but now she acquiesced meekly to Peter's choice. "Non-fattening," he was saying, "after all that spaghetti. Not that you need to watch your diet." His eyes scanned her figure approvingly.

"You don't have to overwhelm me with flattery," said Martina. "I'll take the role you're offering me—gladly, to be honest. I've always had a yen for the theatre, but I never hoped to be an actress. Coaching my high school class is as far as I hoped to get, but I get a bang out of that."

"That's rather pitiable. What a dull life you must lead if that's your idea of a thrill. Frankly, this crummy town, your little dramatic group and all, seem to me the jumping off place to nowhere. I'm wondering what made me take on this assignment. I foresee a summer of vast discomfort."

"But the room Mrs. Davis gave you isn't bad, is it?" asked Martina anxiously.

"The room is all right. I never care what kind of pad I have anyway." Peter dismissed Mrs. Davis' best room with scorn. "It's the rest of this setup that seems so dreary. I must have been out of my mind to dream of a tryout with a high school crowd."

Martina had run out of encouraging remarks. Skip it, she said to herself. But aloud she inquired: "What time does the session start tomorrow?"

"Ten o'clock is early enough," said Peter.

After dinner, Kate's mother was busy with a fashion magazine.

"Here's an easy way to make a summer evening wrap," she said, looking up at Kate, who was sitting on the window seat. "You need something; you've about worn that sequined sweater of yours to shreds."

Kate came over to look at the picture of a girl wearing a two-toned wrap that was scarcely more than a shoulder covering.

"Dreamy," she agreed.

"There's a piece of yellow satin that would look just right with the maize nylon of your class day dress," Mrs. Scott went on. "For a lining— let's see now—that length of shrimp pink satin I was going to use for a sofa cushion. I've been saving it a long time, and the color wouldn't go too well with this room anyway. I bought it because it was a remnant, too cheap to pass up."

Kate pulled up a footstool and perched on it at her mother's feet while she examined the picture of the wrap and glanced at the directions for making it. The model was wearing the wrap so that it left one shoulder alluringly bare. The sleeves, ending just below the elbow, were turned back to show the lining in a contrasting color, and the same effect was achieved at the front of the wrap.

"I'm mad about it," Kate told her mother. "You know, Mom, this is going to be a very important summer in my life, a turning point. It may lead to a stage career faster than I'd hoped. Anyway, it's a step in the right direction. Did I tell you the New York director arrived today?"

Kate had already told her mother this news, though omitting mention of the unfortunate encounter at the gas station. Now, however, after a slight hesitation, she told Mrs. Scott what had occurred.

"I'm worried, Mom. If Mr. Howard holds it against me that I was disagreeable about the accident, he may not want to help me get started on the stage. He may think I'm stupid or something. I've been wondering: If I called him up to apologize, would it make a better impression?"

"Definitely, no," said Mrs. Scott. "He has probably forgotten the whole incident by now. If he's from New York, it's likely this is not the first time somebody has bumped his car."

Kate looked dubious. At that moment the phone rang. She leaped up to answer it so quickly that she kicked the footstool over in her haste. Maybe Mr. Howard—

"Hi!" she called liltingly into the phone.

"Hi." The answering voice was Gil's. Kate's heart, which had skipped a beat, resumed its normal pace.

"The night is young," said Gil, "and there's what looks like a hot film at the Star. They say it's terrif."

"Why wouldn't they? They want to sell tickets."

"Gosh, what's with you, Kate?" demanded Gil. "You always like the movies."

"The living theatre intersts me now."

"But," spluttered Gil, "there's no living theatre in Clyde's Gap, and the nearest summer theatre is fifty miles away. Anyhow, you used to say that you get acting ideas from the movies, even if they're oldies."

"Well, thanks for asking me, Gil," said Kate languidly, "but tonight is out of the question. Mom is making me a new wrap, and I want to help her."

Mrs. Scott, hearing this statement, looked up from her sewing in surprise, then smiled to herself. Poor Gil, she thought. But she was serious when Kate returned.

"If you don't need me, Mom," said Kate, without even asking if she could be of any assistance, "I'll go up and get my things together for tomorrow. Mr. Howard didn't say what time to be there, but we're all planning to be at the barn at seven or thereabouts. I'll just take up a couple of these fashion magazines, if you don't mind."

Upstairs, she sat down before the triple mirror on her dressing table and studied her face head on. Too bad she was so tan. Hollywood stars, she had read, were sometimes cautioned against tanning, if they were to play a part that required that their skin be unbronzed. What kind of part was she to be asked to play? she wondered. It would help her if she knew, so that she could try out suitable hair styles. She fluttered the pages of one of the fashion magazines, looking for suggestions for new hair-dos.

She liked the puffed bang effect, low over the forehead, caught at one side by what the magazine called a cockade. A bow would do as well. Kate rummaged through a drawer, found a suitable ribbon and pinned a little bow at the side of her head. She frowned in the mirror at the result. Suppose hers was to be a sophisticated role, perhaps the role of a young widow? She piled her hair high on top of her head, surveying the effect from all angles, manipulating the wings of her mirror and pausing while she stared critically at the sides and back.

I might as well wait to see what the role calls for, she decided finally, and turned to the make-up pages in the magazine. The beauty consultants evidently considered eye shadow a must.

Should I wear eye shadow tomorrow, when we appear for the cast selections? Kate's mother didn't approve of eye shadow. But appearing for Mr. Howard's inspection tomorrow was not the same as going to school. Besides, Kate's mother belonged to the older generation—thirty-five her last birthday, for heaven's sake—and of course in her days girls didn't use eye shadow. Luckily Kate had her own collection of items for enhancing the eyes. No silver for her lids, though. She bent over the magazine. This fashion expert seemed sold on the subject of silvered lids, or pastel green with a darker green liner. It gave the eyes a wide-open effect, the caption explained. Well, her mother would never let her out of the house with green eyelids.

Kate abandoned the study of eye-make-up in favor of trying out various expressions.

An actress would naturally have to assume many different expressions to be effective in an important role.

These models are showing a lot of different reactions in their faces, she mused, noticing for the first time that the girls modeling the new styles wore different expressions, much as if they were playing roles on the stage.

That model looks like Stella Rand; only Stella is fatter, she thought suddenly. Was there any chance that Stella would be chosen for the star

role in the play? Stella was very popular and had
the advantage of having a banker for a father.
And she had red hair, remarkable red hair.

But she *is* fat, Kate consoled herself. Putting
the threat of Stella's qualifications out of her
mind, Kate devoted herself to assuming a variety
of expressions. Yearning, with her face lifted and
her mouth slightly open. Smiling, with lips shut.
Intensely alert, head a little forward, eyes un-
blinking, fixed.

These models were expressing their feelings
with their whole bodies, she observed presently.
Standing up, leaning over the dressing table to
memorize a pose, she tried one that showed a girl
standing on one foot, the other leg bent backward at the knee, while she put on a slipper that
had evidently come off. It was an awkward pose,
she decided, after she lost both the shoe and her
balance. Another looked very nonchalant; the
girl was standing with one hand on her hip and
the other hand at the back of her head. Kate liked
that. She tried it several times, with her head
thrown back, her mouth open a trifle; smiling,
with her lips closed, frankly laughing. Another
rather good one had the model seated sideways

on a straight chair, her arm thrown over the back of the chair, the hand touching her hair. Kate, with all details attended to, was smiling at her reflection in the mirror when she caught sight of her mother's amazed face in the open doorway.

"The wrap is all basted," Mrs. Scott began, then broke off. "What's so funny?" she asked. "I see you're laughing to yourself in the glass."

"Oh, I was just thinking," said Kate hurriedly. She ran across the room and took the wrap from her mother's hand.

"It's gorgeous." She slipped her arms into it and danced over to her full-length mirror.

"Mom, you're a genius. I look stunning, don't I? I can't wait till Peter sees me in this."

"Peter?" said Evangeline Scott. "You mean Gil, don't you?"

"Gil?" repeated Kate, as if she had never heard the name. "Oh—oh, yes, Gil, of course." Her cheeks were suddenly hot. Mrs. Scott looked at her curiously. Were things getting serious between her daughter and Gil Morehouse? They were both so young.

She sighed and went along the hall to her own room. Kate stood a moment longer, staring at her reflection. Behind her, her own room formed a background for the charming figure she made, but she was seeing herself in an entirely different setting: in some swank restaurant, where the people at all the little tables glanced up as she came forward, followed by a tall dark man whose face she refused to identify.

Chapter 5

At ten o'clock the next morning Peter Howard arrived at the barn. Martina Dawson had preceded him by fifteen minutes, but Kate Scott and the others had been there since seven. Peter was aghast when he heard this.

"No apologies are necessary, sir," said Henry Johnson, in what was for him a courtly manner. Next minute, however, he reverted to his usual style. "These creeps have been kept busy by our understudy Simon Legree, Miss Kate Scott. Haven't you noticed the startling changes around here since yesterday?"

The premises had indeed been transformed. Old crates, boxes and barrels, broken bits of farm equipment, and straggling mounds of hay had disappeared. The floor had been swept clean, the few windows washed; grass had been cut, the path from the road widened, the bushes that encroached on the wide front doors cut back.

Peter surveyed the disheveled crowd. "You've worked wonders," he assured them. "I'm not a big-word guy, but I'm going to use one now. Performance-wise, you're stupendous. Now if you'll all comb the hay out of your hair and wash your hands at Farmer Reynolds' pump I see across the road, we'll get to the try-outs pronto. You girl with the red hair—want to borrow my comb?"

Kate knew it. That Stella Rand, fat or not, was always singled out for attention when there was a man around. Bob Morehouse stepped forward, however, just as Mr. Howard was reaching in his shirt pocket for his comb.

"Don't bother, sir," said Bob. "I've got a comb. Stella can use mine, or—how about it, Stella, I'll use it for you." Before Stella had time to do more than giggle, Bob was combing the hay out of her really magnificent thick, gold-red hair. Kate looked on morosely. Peter Howard glanced at her and did a quick double-take.

"Kate Scott," he called, "when you wash your

hands, better wash your face, too. Your make-up seems to have gotten out of control."

Martina Dawson flashed him a reproachful look as Kate made a quick dash for the pump. Someone had already fixed a small mirror on the side of the old wooden well-house, and Kate stared at her face in horror. She had made up carefully before leaving the house at six-thirty— her mother was not up yet. But in the heat and grime of the clean-up job on the barn, her blue eye shadow, black mascara, scarlet lipstick and pale powder, applied thickly in hope of overcoming her deep tan, had all run and merged into a clownish vari-colored mask. Using her handkerchief, Kate scrubbed at her face furiously.

The heel! The cheap heel! she stormed to herself. Why, he isn't even a Broadway director. Off-Broadway stuff, that's all. She caught her breath in a sob and quickly turned it into a cough. Someone was coming—Gil.

"Come on, Kate," he said; "they're already reading for roles."

"Let them," retorted Kate. "I'm going home. I wouldn't dream of acting in a play that square wrote."

Gil stared at her, aghast. "But the whole thing was your idea, Kate."

"That was before I got a look at Mr. Peter Howard. Where Miss Dawson dug him up—"

"He sent me to get you. He says he thinks he wants you for the juvenile lead. And because you'll be in every scene, just about, he says he wants you there while the others are reading."

"That's a laugh. He doesn't know a thing about me—except that my face was dirty."

"But he does think you have—what did he call it?—drive. That's what makes for good acting, he says: drive. The way you made everybody step around and get the barn into shape this morning proved that you've got what it takes, he said. Henry Johnson went around after you left, showing him everything that had been done and telling him that if it hadn't been for you none of us would have raised a finger. And you know what Mr. Howard said?"

Kate shook her head.

"He said, and I quote, 'A girl who can work her make-up into a mess and not give a hoot, that's the girl I had in mind when I wrote the juvenile lead part in my play. And from where I sit—or stand rather—that girl is Kate Scott."

Kate eyed Gil doubtfully. He wouldn't make up anything like that. Gil seized her hand.

"We've got to *run!*" he cried. Kate, laughing, began to run obligingly, and they flew across the road. Inside the barn, Peter Howard was handing around a few typewritten sheets. Martina Dawson was holding one, and Peter gave Kate another as she came in.

"Now keep in mind that the audience is interested in the character each of you plays—not you personally. When I assign your roles, finally, I want each of you to study them, to lose yourselves in them, off stage as well as on. Be the character you are going to play; think yourself into *being* that character, even at home. You can explain what you're doing to your parents, if they start giving you peculiar looks."

"Wait till Father gets an eyeful of his darling Stella as a prim, somewhat timid young lady mincing into the dining room for dinner," shrieked Stella Rand, who had been reading the notes on her typewritten sheet.

"Silence!" thundered Peter Howard. Kate jumped. Gil grinned. Stella pouted. Peter ignored them for a moment, looking down at the pages in his hand. "Bob Morehouse!" he called. Bob lounged into view in the open door. "Here," said Peter. "Read this." He indicated several lines with his finger. "As soon as he finishes, you, Martina, answer him. And while she's still speaking, you, Kate, interrupt her. There's where you start."

The reading proceeded for the next half-hour, constantly interrupted by Peter's directions and comments.

"All right; knock it off for five minutes," he growled at the end of that time, throwing Martina a despairing look. She moved over to stand beside him when he went outside and leaned against the side of the barn.

"They're nervous," she said soothingly. "After this break they'll pull themselves together and do better. You'll see."

"My play!" groaned Peter. "Stillborn!"

"Now you're being silly," said Martina. "And you're not fair to the kids."

Peter laughed. "Martina of the level head!" he murmured. "Thank heaven you're neither a playwright nor an actress, baby." He broke off at

Martina's outraged expression. "I only meant," he floundered, "not a professional actress. You're doing great in this play, really great."

"By contrast, I suppose," said Martina coldly.

"Don't go icy on me, Tina," Peter begged. "You know I depend on you to keep me from blowing my top. You know the setup here; you can keep the kids in line—and me too," he finished humbly.

Martina patted his arm. "There, there," she murmured, "are the disrespectful teen-agers spoiling the gifted playwright's inspired play?"

Peter laughed. "See what I mean?" he asked. "A few minutes with you and I'm back in the groove again."

As Martina had predicted, things went smoothly when readings were resumed. The group had lost some of its self-consciousness and tried hard to follow Peter's suggestions. At noon they paused long enough to eat the sandwiches they had all brought, at Martina's suggestion, and soon afterward Peter began assigning roles.

Martina Dawson was to be the star in an older woman role; Kate was set for the juvenile female lead; Stella Rand was the second juvenile lead.

Peter selected Bob Morehouse for the male lead.

"But he isn't even one of us," a youth with a butch haircut protested loudly. "He's not even in our school."

"That's right. He's not eligible," someone seconded the objection.

"But he's Gil Morehouse's brother, and Gil's working hard on this project," a girl put in.

"And Stella Rand has fallen for him."

"What's that got to do with giving him the best role in the show?" demanded the first speaker.

"Who's bank-rolling this production?" demanded the boy who had observed that Stella Rand had fallen for Bob. "Stella Rand's banker father, that's who," he answered himself. The rest of the group fell silent and, though there were hostile glances in Bob's direction, there were no more objections raised.

Minor roles had been assigned and Peter was about to declare the cast complete when he said to Martina, in a worried aside: "I think I'll have to rewrite my play slightly. There's an older man —a farmer—and I can't see any of these boys looking anything but ridiculous in the part, even with make-up."

Kate, nearby, overheard the remark. "What's the matter with Farmer Reynolds?" she asked. "If the role doesn't call for too much acting ability—"

"Actually, it's nothing but a walk-on part," explained Peter, "but it's necessary to give color to a couple of the scenes. Farmer Reynolds— that's the guy who's been keeping an eye on us from across the road nearly all day, I take it?— could fit into the show, even without make-up."

"That old coot wouldn't lift a finger to help if all our lives depended on it," said Stella Rand, who had come up in time to hear the end of the discussion.

"Stella!" said Martina Dawson reprovingly.

Stella made a face, which Martina pretended not to see.

"Maybe," said Kate, "if you'd ask him, Mr. Howard. He is letting us use his barn."

"Yeah," said Henry Johnson, "but look at the remodeling job he's getting in return!"

"All the same," persisted Kate, "he has been spending a lot of time watching us over here. He may be really interested in the idea of a play."

Peter considered. "You may have something there, Kate," he said finally. "I haven't much hope, but there can't be any harm in giving it the old school try."

"Just inviting him to join the cast may change his attitude toward us," Kate added. "As it is, we never know when he's going to call a halt to our renovations and stymie us."

"Well, here goes." Peter made a show of squaring his shoulders as he marched out of the door and headed across the road. He was back in a short time and faced the anxious troupe, who stood with fingers ostentatiously crossed, their hands held out in front of them.

"Well, kids, our cast is now complete," he told the group. "Mr. Reynolds has consented to play himself in our production."

"Hooray!" shouted Henry Johnson, and the others promptly joined in the cheer: "Hip, hip, hooray!"

There were still endless details to the business of producing a play, Kate found, when Peter Howard sat down chummily on an overturned egg box and explained that it was necessary to appoint committees to be in charge of publicity, poster making, ticket selling and furniture collecting. Volunteers were called for.

"I'll sell tickets," offered Stella Rand. "Bob Morehouse will help me, he says."

"Fine!" said Peter. "Any more offers? This is a very important committee and we need at least six members."

Four hands shot up, and Peter took the names of the two boys and two girls who were offering their services. Kate offered to take over the job of getting in touch with local newspapers and arranging for the town's stores to display the posters which the poster committee, as yet unnamed, would provide.

"I think we can carry our publicity campaign farther afield," said Peter. "There are nearby towns where we can hope for customers, and all the summer hotels around offer potential audiences if they are approached properly. I've had some experience in this sort of thing myself—mostly in the city, of course—and I consider myself quite an old hand at it. I suggest you head the publicity committee, Kate, and if you'd care to have me on your committee—"

"I couldn't hope for that," said Kate, "but if you really have the time—"

"Then that's settled," Peter said briskly. "Now let's see—the poster making—" A half-dozen hands waved wildly in the air.

"The art courses are very popular in our school," explained Martina. "We have some very promising artists, too, I understand from the staff."

"Will you take over the poster committee, Martina, and sign up the owners of all these hands?" Peter inquired.

Martina nodded and went about taking down names for her own and the other committees. Gil Morehouse had to leave to get on with his paper route. "Put me down for publicity," he said casually as he passed Martina. "Being a newspaperman—" He grinned at Kate and gave her a mock salute. She glanced hastily away, just in time to catch Henry Johnson's wink, which she appeared not to notice.

"Well, that about winds up the first day's work," Peter told them, after a few more details had been discussed. "Now listen, everybody! No need to get here at seven in the A.M. hereafter.

We'll start rehearsals at ten, knock off about one, and from then on the various committees can go to work. Scene painters and so on may proceed with their work during rehearsals, providing they don't hammer too loud."

Kate watched him as he went toward his car and slipped behind the wheel. A good half of the cast piled into Henry Johnson's heap—his own name for the beat-up car he drove—and Martina Dawson went off in her roadster. Kate walked slowly to her own car, an idea forming in her mind.

If she hadn't brought her own car, if she had walked to Farmer Reynolds' place, perhaps Peter Howard would have offered to drive her home. It wasn't really much of a walk from her house.

"The exercise will do me good," she decided.

There might be an opportunity to discuss chances for a real stage career for her, too. Besides, this Peter Howard was quite a guy. One couldn't help liking him.

Chapter 6

As Kate had predicted, once Farmer Reynolds was a part of the cast, there was no further argument over changes in the barn. On the contrary, the old farmer did his farm chores early and was underfoot from morning till night. His wife called to him from time to time and, while he always answered, Kate noticed that it often took him fifteen or twenty minutes before he actually crossed the road.

Even the director had to concede that Farmer Reynolds was a great help. He knew just how much voltage the cable would bear, and he helped the boys string the extension cords.

" 'Course y'know," he admonished, "ya gotta get the electrician of Clyde's Gap to give the okay so it's all legal-like, but ain't no use paying him for what we can do ourselves. When it comes to that, I know as much about wiring as Hank Bonnell, and if he don't give us the okay, or hesitates about it, I maybe know a way to change his mind."

"The thing I'm worried about," the director confessed, "is the underpinning of the floor. This is a big barn, and we should have at least a hundred people at each performance. Also, we've got to cut a couple of doors for exits in case of fire. I don't expect any trouble," he added hastily, "but it's the law, and we must be sure we are doing the right thing, even if the show runs for only a short time."

"I'll show the boys how to cut between the uprights," the farmer said, moving off briskly, and Peter turned to Kate with a comradely grin.

"Bless you for having me ask him to be part of the cast," he said sincerely. "If he had fought our ideas, instead of working with us, we wouldn't have been able to put on the show this summer."

Kate nodded absently. She was watching as Stella reluctantly broke off her apparently earnest discussion with Bob Morehouse and started back outside. All the girls had been assigned to reconditioning and repainting the "flats" which would eventually be lashed together to form an interior. The boys were concentrating on getting the wiring and carpentry done, so that the stage could be erected with all possible speed. But Stella, as far as Kate could see, took her assignment lightly and spent more time talking to Bob than she did in the field outside.

"The title of the play is *When Morning Comes*," the director had explained, "and the action takes place about 1912—before TV, that is; before radio. So when this actress and her agent get stranded in a lonely country farmhouse, the farmer's son—that's Bob Morehouse— is swept off his feet by the glamorous star. The situation makes for some good light comedy lines, but we must indicate by the background just how poor and unworldly the farmer and his son are.

"That is why I want the flats painted that particular shade of bilious green," he went on. "After they are finished and dry, we might even put in some brown streaks, to indicate the roof has leaked and stained the walls."

"You haven't heard a word I said," Peter accused Kate, who was looking after Stella as she reluctantly left the barn. "Don't worry so about your friend—she can take care of herself."

"I'm not so much worried about Stella as I am about her father," Kate admitted. "He wouldn't like it a little bit if he found out she was seeing so much of Bob Morehouse."

"Why? He seems like a nice enough fellow."

"Oh, he is!" Kate said hastily. "He's very nice. But it isn't good enough for Mr. Rand. After all, he's the banker—in fact, he's paying your salary," Kate could not resist adding. "Bob was involved in a boyhood scrape a few years back and that, added to the fact he's not the son of anyone important, puts him out of the running, as far as Stella's father is concerned."

Peter gave a low whistle. "So that's the way the cookie crumbles," he said lightly. "I wish Mr. Rand luck in trying to control his fiery, redheaded daughter. Bob—in fact, both of the Morehouse boys—are good-looking kids. But I won't have you worrying about it. You are the lead in the show, together with Martina. You've got to keep looking and feeling your best. . . . Say, let's get out of here. That hammering and sawing is enough to drive anyone crazy."

They walked out into a late afternoon that was typical of June; just pleasantly warm and with a breeze that hinted of late lilacs and early roses. Kate sank gratefully onto the "Deacon's bench" that was placed along one side of the barn, and Peter, with a heart-felt sigh, sat down beside her.

"I thought it was tough working with professionals," he said finally. "But never before have I had to build the theatre. Even in college the background stuff was there. All we had to do were the scenery and costumes; there were always plenty of art students and girls studying home economics to take care of little things like that. By the way, how's the brigade to collect old furniture coming along?"

Kate confessed that she had been busy studying her part and had not checked with the furniture committee. She understood, however, that they were all working hard, and the ticket committee and her own publicity committe were planning on doing a good job, too.

"How do you know so much about it, if you've been busy?"

"I was talking to Gil Morehouse the other

night." Kate felt her color rising as Peter looked at her keenly.

"The Morehouse boys sure have a way with the ladies," Peter commented dryly. "I've been wondering what became of Gil."

"He was here earlier," Kate assured him, "but he had to leave at four-thirty to deliver the evening papers. He's on all three committees, but he finds time to work on the wiring, too."

"More than a triple threat lad," Peter murmured.

Kate ignored the comment. "I doubt if he'll be back tonight; it must be about five o'clock now. When are we leaving?"

"At five o'clock," Peter said, glancing at his watch. "It's two minutes of, so suppose you go and tell them to knock off. No, wait a second." He caught Kate's wrist as she stood up. "In the interest of keeping up the morale of an important member of the cast, I suggest we have dinner somewhere around here—not in Clyde's Gap—and talk about something else for a change. It will do you good."

"Why, thank you, I think that would be fine," Kate said delightedly. "Shall we ask Martina?"

"We'll ask no one but ourselves," Peter said shortly. "Anyway, I happen to know Martina is tied up for the evening—a ladies' sewing circle or something. Where can we go?"

"If you like Italian food, there's a small restaurant on the Starlight Route. They even have a dance floor and a juke box."

Peter appeared to consider, but Kate had an idea he was not too anxious to follow her suggestion. "It's not quite what I had in mind," he said at last. "I was told by a friend of mine who has spent his vacations up this way that there's sort of a Swiss chalet—"

"The Berkshire Chalet!"

"That's it. How far away is it from here?"

"Only about thirty-five miles," Kate said dreamily. "But you don't want to go there. They have a real orchestra and marvelous food and a dreamy dance floor, but it's very very expensive. Or so I've heard. I've never been there."

"You'll be there tonight," Peter promised. "You let me worry about the cost. Now dust inside and tell them to get packed up. What on earth goes on?"

From the direction of the road came a lusty

roaring sound that grew in volume and mingled with the rattles and wheezes of an old and well-used car. It took a few minutes for the vehicle to get to the barn. Kate had already identified it as Gil's old heap, and the singer as Gil himself.

"Gil has quite a voice that he can be heard above the rattle of that car,'" Peter commented. "But what on earth has he got on top?"

Gil had brought his car to a quivering stop, and Kate and Peter stared at the four legs of some piece of furniture that reached helplessly toward the sky. The "carpenters" and "electricians" had come to the door of the barn, and now they started shouting at Gil:

"Come on, boy!" "Swing it, you creep!" "What's the matter, Gil—lost your voice?"

Gil stepped out of the car by the simple method of throwing his long legs over the door. He jumped to the ground and stood for a moment in silence.

"If he opens the door, it falls off," Kate explained to Peter in a whisper.

Suddenly Gil stepped up the rhythm of the opera. Doing a step that was half Calypso and half twist," he danced up and down before his audience, snapping his fingers like castenets.

"*Santa Luciiiia*—

"*Santa Luciiiia*—

"*Santa Luciiia*—

"*Santa Lucia.*"

He had made his voice softer and softer, until the little dance he was doing dominated the performance. At the last, his voice, now almost a whisper, trailed off into the silence and the dance came to an abrupt halt. Those who were watching broke into applause, and Gil shouted at them:

"Cut it out, you lunkheads. Come over here and help me unload this settee. Since Mr. Howard is still here, maybe he'll tell me whether he wants to use it for a prop or not."

Amiably, the boys came over to the car, and the small love seat was soon standing on its legs in the dusty driveway. The upholstery had once been yellow, but now was faded in streaks, and there was a small corner ripped at one side. The frame was sturdy and carved, however, and the design was graceful.

"I'm sorry," Gil apologized to Peter, "but this is the best I could find. When I told Mrs. Cameron that if you took it you would pay ten dollars for it, she couldn't wait until I had it loaded on."

"I should think so!" Stella had left her work painting flats, and she and the other girls were grouped in front of the boys. "Mrs. Cameron wouldn't get a dollar and a half for that thing at an auction."

"That's just what I had in mind, Gil," Peter said with satisfaction. "It's in pretty good condition, but we can soon fix that." He stepped over and picked up the torn corner; the fabric ripped a foot more, and those who were watching laughed.

"You sure made it antique," Stella commented.

"All right, you kids," Peter said quietly. "Put this in the barn and get packed up to leave. Tomorrow you've really got to work. I want that stage finished by next week."

Kate followed him to the car, a small sports model that was the envy of every boy in town. Peter made only one remark on the way down the mountainside:

"Where did Gil Morehouse learn to swing opera music?" he inquired.

"I guess he just made it up," Kate answered.

She had never thought about it before. "He knows lots of operas, and we always ask him to do something for us when we have picnics or cook-outs. We think he's great," she added loyally.

When they drew up before Kate's house, Peter broke the silence once more. "I'll call for you in an hour," he told her. "Okay?"

"Oh, yes," Kate agreed at once. She added in a faltering voice: "But there's one thing. I suppose you'll think it's kind of childish, but Mom always asks me to bring my date into the house when I first go out with him, so that she can meet him and know whom I'm with. Do you mind?"

"Of course not," Peter said at once. "On the contrary, I heartily approve. You are much too pretty to be dating someone your mother doesn't know. Do you think she'll approve?"

"But yes," Kate said, grinning. "How could she not?"

Yet when Kate told her mother about her thrilling plans for the evening, Evangeline Scott looked at her daughter thoughtfully. There were times, she reflected, when it was hard to know how to bring up a teen-age girl in this day and age. Her own mother and father had laid down a strict code of behavior when she was sixteen, but it was hard to apply their principles to this era.

"And I can wear the dress I wore to the Junior Prom and the wrap you made me. Oh, Mom, I didn't know when I'd get a chance to dress up again. This is just like a dream—it's so right. And the Berkshire Chalet! None of the boys have the kind of money to go there—"

"That's just it," Kate's mother interrupted her daughter firmly. "If this man has already made a name for himself in his profession, he must be quite a bit older than you are. The boys and girls you ordinarily go around with are in your class and about your age. You've known most of them several years. I know their mothers and fathers. Going out with an older man who is making a career for himself in New York is another story."

"Oh, Mom, don't be so stuffy," Kate protested. "He *is* older than I am. He's about twenty-six or twenty-seven. But Peter fits right in with the crowd. He was one of us in no time at all. He may seem like an older man to you, but in the theatrical world, he's a boy wonder. He's a genius, Mom, and the same rules don't apply."

"Maybe not," Evangeline Scott agreed. "But just the same, you've only known him a short time. You don't know what his background is; you don't even know if he's married."

Kate felt suddenly deflated. It was quite true; she didn't know Peter's marital status. She had simply assumed that he was not married, but he had never said so. Martina Dawson had never spoken of Peter's personal life. But having reached a low point, Kate rallied.

"I may not have known him long," she said defensively, "but Martina Dawson was in his drama class in college. I'm sure she wouldn't bring anyone to Clyde's Gap who was a scoundrel! Mom, you aren't going to say I can't go, are you?"

"No," Evangeline Scott said slowly. "You've already promised to keep the date, and I'll trust you to take care of yourself tonight. But I *do* want to meet him, and I *don't* want you to make any more dates until you know a little about his background."

Kate gave her mother a quick hug, and her spirtis soared. What her mother said made sense. But tonight at least was hers to enjoy. She would put her hair on top of her head; it really made her look quite a bit older and sophisticated. She glanced at the clock and gave a gasp of dismay.

"Oh, Mom! He'll be here in less than an hour. Now don't worry about a thing, Mom. I can take care of myself."

Kate ran up the stairs, feeling that she had wings on her feet. Who would ever think that she would be going to dinner at the Berkshire Chalet with Peter S. Howard, brilliant young director and playwright of the smart New York theatrical world?

Chapter 7

Kate stole a glance at the stern profile across the perfectly appointed table for two at the Berkshire Chalet and reflected that her escort was really quite handsome. He looked at her suddenly, and again she felt that peculiar thrill—almost like a shiver—that his piercing glance always evoked. She looked down hastily at her menu, but the over-size list of foods, without prices, made absolutely no sense.

She had dreamed of walking into the swank restaurant and choosing the dishes she preferred with an air of sophistication. But ever since Kate had first glimpsed the Chalet, its stucco and timbered structure set on the highest hill, she had found it impossible to pretend. Now she gave up and folded the large menu card with finality.

"Please order for me, Peter. I've never seen so many different kinds of food listed. Generally I have a choice of either hamburgers or hot dogs when I'm eating out."

Peter's smile seemed to illuminate the whole room. "You are a contradictory person, Kate," he said, shaking his head. "One minute you are perfectly poised; then all at once you are entirely frank and honest, as only a high school senior could be."

"I might as well admit it," Kate said, glancing around the softly lighted room. "I'm all shook up about being in this glamorous place—with a professional director from New York."

Peter sighed in mock despair. "Ah, me! And I was in hopes we could forget all about the theatre and rehearsals and rebuilding Farmer Reynolds' barn and just talk about *us*. You've been so busy trying to put this idea across, I haven't gotten to know you. Of course I know you're beautiful, and Martina tells me you're a wonderful actress, but I don't know the real you."

"There's very little more to find out about me, although I think you have been a little too flattering in your description. We'll get around to me after a while, but in the meantime I'd like to talk about you."

"I'll give our order, and then you can fire questions at me a mile a minute," Peter promised. He called the waiter, dressed appropriately in green knee pants, a green bolero and a white frilled shirt. While they discussed the meal, Kate reflected on the surprising events of the last hour.

She had been ready a few minutes early and was satisfied that the yellow chiffon was very becoming and that the upswept hairdo made her look at least two years older. Her mother, too, was pleased with her ensemble, she knew, although her smile had seemed a little sad.

"Don't mind me," her mother had said apologetically. "It's hard for a mother to realize her daughter is growing up so fast. There's the bell. I will say for him: your young man is right on time."

Kate was entirely pleased with Peter's reaction when she opened the door. He pretended that he did not know her and must have come to the wrong house. She reached out finally, pulled him over the threshold and then led him sedately into the living room.

Evangeline's small, square figure was standing beside the fireplace, stiffly erect. She looked pleasantly interested in meeting her daughter's escort, although her manner was not cordial. Then, it seemed to Kate, everything changed suddenly.

"Mom," she said quietly, "this is Peter Howard, who is directing our summer group. My mother, Mr. Howard."

Mrs. Scott held out her hand, murmured, "Mr. Howard," and suddenly her manner brightened. "Peter Howard?" she said. "At one time in my life the name was familiar. Let's see—Howard's Hitches. Do they mean anything to you?"

Peter seemed taken aback. "How did you know? I mean, that's the family business. But very few people connect me with it."

"Probably I wouldn't either," said Mrs. Scott, with a warm smile, "except that my husband used those hitches in his work. At one time I heard about one of Howard's Hitches every night of my life."

"What on earth are Howard's Hitches?" demanded Kate.

"They are metal fastenings that join something movable to something else that pulls it," explained Peter with a grin. "Was it a trucking business your husband had?" he asked Mrs. Scott, who nodded.

"Please don't let the word get around," Peter said earnestly. "Dad wanted me to go into the family business, but I've been trying to make my way in the theatre. If I admitted I was the son of a successful manufacturer, I'd never get any credit for getting along on my own."

"You must follow your own star," agreed Mrs. Scott. "And I mustn't keep you talking. Run along and have a good time."

On the drive to the Berkshire Chalet, and ever since their arrival there, Kate had managed to keep the conversation light and inconsequential. But her mind kept going back to that scene in the living room when her mother's whole attitude had changed.

"Hi! Where are you? You look as if you'd taken off for the moon," Peter said suddenly. "I've given our order, and the orchestra is taking its place at the end of the room. If there's anything serious you want to say before we start dancing and eating, you'd better start now."

"From what Mother said back home," Kate began, making no apology for her directness, "I gather that your father is a big businessman, a wealthy man."

Peter shrugged. "The term wealthy is comparative. Dad has been a successful businessman for the last twenty years, and he is a shrewd investor. But his way of life isn't for me. I feel as if I were born for the theatre. I haven't made much headway so far, but I've still got a while to go before Dad calls a halt. I'm hoping that this play will get some recognition. Of course, if it moves to Broadway, or sells to the movies, that's it. I'll have it made."

"Why did you say that about your Dad calling a halt?"

"I have an agreement with him. He subsidizes me for another year. If I don't have something to show for my efforts by that time, I'll go back home and go into the business. I'll play fair."

Kate felt somewhat resentful. The waiter had put in front of them a fruit cocktail nestled in a silver chalice filled with cracked ice, and she dipped into its cool sweetness. "You certainly kept your secret well," she commented. "According to Miss Dawson, you had to be guaranteed the five hundred dollars before you came to

Clyde's Gap."

"You think I should have come for free?" Peter demanded.

"We've even started a coach's fund!" Kate could not keep a note of bitterness from creeping into her voice. "We all contribute something from our allowances so that you won't find it too much of a hardship to work with us."

Peter nodded. "Yes, Tina told me about it. I'm sorry you had to find out I wasn't a starving hanger-on in the theatrical profession, and I hope you won't give me away."

"Why shouldn't I?" Kate demanded. "Why should we go on pitying you and giving up part of our allowances?"

"You will be doing everyone connected with this project a great disservice," Peter said grimly. "It is not too soon for you to learn that no one appreciates something for free. Tell everyone that I can afford to work for nothing and you'll soon see a great change in their attitude. They'll think of this summer theatre as being just for fun and they won't listen to me. If I criticize their acting, they'll challenge my right to tell them any of the facts of show business."

Kate thought for a minute and then had to agree that Peter was right. Even Martina Dawson would find it hard to control the future seniors if they found out that she had misrepresented Peter's place in the theatrical world.

"If you're thinking that Martina Dawson would be under fire for recommending me, you're perfectly right," Peter said as if he were reading her thoughts. "However, Tina knows nothing about Howard's Hitches, and she would be as surprised as anyone to hear I wasn't a struggling theatrical hack. But no one would believe she *didn't* know.

"She wouldn't be the only adult affected," Peter said, his eyes flashing. "Stella's father would demand his money back. Farmer Reynolds would ask a steep fee for the barn. In some strange way, they would assume that *they* were doing *me* a favor, and your whole attempt to do something serious in summer theatre work would fall flat on its face."

"I won't say anything," Kate said in a subdued voice. "You are perfectly right, of course. At our age, we are all given too much; we've got to learn that we must pay for what is worthwhile."

One of Peter's rare smiles flashed at her, and he rose from his chair. "Enough of this serious talk," he said decisively ."I see our waiter approaching with the salad. Let's get in a dance while he's mixing and serving it."

Kate was swept onto the dance floor with smooth, rhythmic ease and gave herself up wholly to the enjoyment of the music, the festive air of the guests and the perfect timing of her partner. She danced well, and she enjoyed dancing with Gil and Henry Johnson and most of the other boys in the crowd. But dancing with Peter was a new experience. It was like dancing on air!

The salad was ready when they returned to the table, and as they started to eat, the waiter brought up a serving stand and started to carve a roast duck. The appetizing aroma of the orange sauce and the steaming vegetables made Kate realize she was ravenously hungry. She waited until Peter was served, however, before she picked up her fork.

"This is but heavenly!" she exclaimed at the first mouthful of duck. "But I don't understand this vegetable."

"Heart of artichoke," Peter said gaily.

"I'm glad the coach's fund doesn't have to pay for this," Kate said with a twinkle.

Peter laughed and began to tell her of his experiences as an aspiring actor, director and would-be successful aspirant in the theatrical world. Because most of the men and women in the same category were operating on a shoestring, Peter felt honor bound to share their hardships as well as their joys.

This had led to complications; he was not used to drinking cup after cup of muddy coffee in a greasy diner or restaurant. He was not accustomed to talking until four o'clock in the morning and sleeping until noon. He had a passion for neatness, and whenever he invited a fellow worker to share his "pad," he usually made some excuse to dart up to his rooms and throw things around a bit.

"I had indigestion for the first month," Peter said with a wry smile. "Then I learned to sneak into a really good restaurant uptown, where the theatrical crowd didn't go, and get myself a square meal once in a while. But for a while the road was plenty rough."

Kate was looking at him with rapt attention. She felt it was a privilege to get such an intimate glimpse of life back-stage, or off-stage. "It sounds so glamorous," she said at last. "It must be worth the experience, even if you go hungry."

Peter looked at her with a wry smile. "Maybe I've been gilding the lily a little bit. I assure you the theatrical business is sometimes heartbreaking, always discouraging and in any case highly competitive. I've been in on more postmortems for turkeys."

"Turkeys? In New York?" Kate questioned.

"A theatrical term for a play that is a flop," Peter explained impatiently. "Maybe an actor has been out of work for a long time; then he gets a part—perhaps just a bit part—and he gets more and more enthusiastic during rehearsals. He can even see his name in lights on Broadway! Then comes opening night. The critics are unanimous in their scorn and predict the play will close before the end of the week. So he's out of work again, maybe for another long stretch. Back to making the rounds of the casting offices; back to black coffee and hamburger or just black coffee."

"It still sounds plenty exciting," Kate insisted.

"I know it must be hard work and discouraging at times. But even so, when you get a break—really get into the big time, I mean—" Kate was proud of her knowledge of this term.

"You've got to make your own breaks, infant," Peter said with a wry smile. "Oh, I know you've read about how somebody was discovered in a small part and went on to become a big star; or how a young singer stepped onto the stage and stopped the show. But let me point out that these stories appear *after* the actor is a star. Usually they are just a press agent's dream."

"You can't make me believe it's nothing but hardship," Kate said stubbornly. "After all, there are agents who scout around and find good parts for you, and arrange about salary and—" She stopped at Peter's laugh of frank delight.

"It's refreshing to meet anyone so naïve," he said as he subsided into an occasional chuckle. "No important agent will be bothered with someone trying to break into the theatre; they are all concerned only with big names, the acknowledged stars. My child, if you are planning on a professional career, you have much to learn. Maybe before then you will decide it isn't worth it," he added as a somber afterthought.

There was a roll of drums from the orchestra, and the master of ceremonies stepped forward. As the patrons quieted, he stepped to the microphone and said with a grin:

"Does anyone here know how to do the Twist?"

There was a burst of laughter and applause from the patrons in which Kate and Peter joined.

"Ah! I can see you are the Smart Set," the M.C. said with mock seriousness. "So I am sure you will be glad to hear that we are going to hold a Twist contest. But the rules are slightly different from those of the usual contests. It will be an elimination dance, but you will eliminate yourselves. When you can no longer take it, you drop out and return to your table. There will be no one to tap you on the shoulder.

"Now the prizes," he continued, "are really something special. The first couple to drop out wins the booby prize. The last couple remaining on the floor wins the grand prize. Come on," he urged; "let's go!"

Kate and Peter joined the surge toward the dance floor and soon were twisting in earnest.

After only a few minutes, a matronly woman and her frail escort gave up and, amid general laughter, left the floor.

"I wonder what the booby prize is," said Kate, enjoying the fun.

"I bribed the headwaiter to find out," Peter confessed. "The booby prize is a silver loving cup; the grand prize is a bottle of liniment."

"But that's not fair," Kate was protesting when she noticed that Peter had come to a full stop and was staring angrily over her head. She looked over her shoulder just in time to see Martina Dawson, in a gay print dance frock, turn back to her tall blond escort. Her cheeks were bright, and Kate wondered how she had managed to achieve such a sleek hairdo, considering her usual flyaway hair.

"I thought you said Miss Dawson had a meeting."

Peter, his face thunderous, did not bother to answer. Instead he took her firmly by the elbow and steered her back to their table. "Let's get out of here," he muttered.

Kate's heart sank. So she owed this evening to a quarrel!

Chapter 8

The Fourth of July was suddenly upon her. Kate was sure that if she lived to be a hundred, she would never forgt the Fourth of July holiday that interrupted rehearsals for *When Morning Comes*. Martina Dawson had gone home to spend the holiday with her parents in Maine.

"I usually go home for the summer," she explained to Peter Howard, when announcing her departure. "But this year, with your play keeping me busy, I haven't taken even a weekend to visit the folks. In a way I'm sorry to leave Clyde's Gap right now. I understand there are big doings afoot."

It was at the end of a day of rehearsal and Kate, standing nearby, overheard Martina talking to Peter. Whatever the reason for their coolness the other night, they seemed to be back to the old status.

"We're sorry to see you go, too," said Peter. "The town won't seem the same with Martina gone, will it, Kate?"

"But it's only for a short time," returned Kate. "We won't have time to miss her—really—before she's back."

Peter gave her what she thought to herself to be a "funny" look, but he made no answer. Maybe he was glad to have Martina out of the way for a time, she was thinking as she helped put away brushes and paint cans. She said good night to Martina and "Happy Holiday," and watched her drive off down the narrow road.

Kate had walked to the barn from her home that morning, hoping, as she had done before, that Peter would notice she was without her car. Her ruse had not been very successful thus far, and she had been slightly irritated at being overlooked by Peter several times and left to hitch a ride with other members of the cast. They usually rode four in a seat. In the case of one particular car which she detested, a couple of the boys sat on the floor and dangled their legs out either side, the car doors being missing.

But tonight Peter Howard saw her standing disconsolately by while she watched her classmates arranging themselves in the last car—exactly like a lot of sardines, she observed mentally.

"Hi, Kate! Where's your car?" Peter called.

"I'm walking," said Kate, gaily. "I don't want to get overweight, you know."

"You—overweight?" Peter scoffed: "Here; hop in."

He flung the door open, and Kate whisked into the seat beside him.

"It's such a short run," she said, and paused so he might suggest that they take a turn around the reservoir or ride through the grounds adjacent to the State Hospital nearby. Both were drives much in favor among the young people of the town, affording as they did certain secluded spots that were suitable for parking. But Peter acted as if he had not heard her.

"I suppose you'll be in the parade tomorrow," he said.

"Of course," said Kate. "All the kids will be— the little ones from the grade school as well as the high school pupils."

"See you then," said Peter, as he let her out in front of her own door.

It must be the difference in their ages, Kate told herself as she went up the walk between her mother's delphiniums and around the house to the back. If only he'd arrange things so that they could see more of each other and he could get to know her—really to know her—he'd realize that a girl of sixteen these days was quite grown up. He's twenty-six, she thought. Ten years between them, if you went by the calendar, but much less if you considered her own mature viewpoint. She wished fervently that she did not have to wear the white shirtwaist and dark blue skirt which had been agreed upon by the girls in her class as their parade uniform. She would have liked to wear her new pink handkerchief linen dress, which was sleeveless, short-skirted and as low in the neck as her mother would permit for street wear.

I'll be surprised if Peter can pick me out in the crowd of white-shirtwaist-and-blue-skirt girls milling around, she told herself in deep discouragement.

But she was wrong. When the parade was over

and all the patriotic songs had been sung, with the whole town joining in, and the wreaths had been laid at the local monuments to war heroes, and finally the town leaders—including Banker Rand—had made ringing but, in Kate's opinion, too lengthy speeches, she was standing in line, with the others, waiting her turn to buy one of the box lunches which had been supplied by one of the nearby summer hotels at cost, when she felt a tap on her shoulder. It was Peter Howard.

"Allow me," he said. "I'll be your stand-in." He shouldered her gently aside, and she laughingly gave up her place to him.

"I'll get the cokes," she said, and went over to the coffee and coke concession, where her mother was helping serve.

"You'll want a box lunch," Mrs. Scott told her, noticing that Kate had nothing in her hands.

"Peter's getting lunches for both of us," the girl said happily. Kate accepted the two coke bottles and, after accepting a pat on her hand from her mother as she handed them out, moved toward the spot where Peter was waiting, the box lunches under his arm.

"You'll ruin them," protested Kate. "Hold

them right side up."

"I assumed they'd be indestructible, like all ready-made picnic lunches." Peter grinned. "Where shall we go to eat them?"

After dismissing several locations as too crowded, too noisy (the band was really hitting it up) or near what looked to him like poison ivy, they finally perched side by side on a huge flat rock. They ate and talked and laughed for a half-hour. Kate thought she had never been happier in her life.

There was a platform erected for dancing at one end of the large open space which was the traditional gathering place for community get-togethers or occasions such as this. Kate, watching the high school crowd cavorting gaily to the lively tunes played by the band, was hoping that Peter would ask her to dance. Then everybody could see that he was interested in her and perhaps begin to speculate on whether or not they were engaged. Then a sudden commotion at the edge of the woods attracted their attention.

"Herbie! Herbie!" a woman was screaming. "Herbie, come here this minute!"

The surrounding crowd took up the cry, and

shouts of "Herbie!" could be heard above the band.

"Kid must be lost, strayed or stolen," said Peter. "Let's investigate."

Others were running from all directions, and Kate and Peter joined them as they swelled the crowd. There were loud questions directed at anybody near, particularly the children.

"Have you seen Herbie, honey?" asked a woman of a little golden-haired girl.

"Who wants to know?" the youngster retorted.

Others were more cooperative. In fact, so many kids claimed to have seen Herbie going that way, or this way, or the other way, alone or with a woman in black or with two men with guns in their hands—young television addicts were very firm about what they had seen—that the adults gave up the interrogation.

"He must have wandered into the woods," one of the men shouted at last, addressing the crowd. "Spread out, folks, and search. He can't be far away, if his mother has only just missed him. How old is he, Mrs. Barnstable?"

"He's just six," the mother sobbed. "Six last

Monday a week."

"All right, everybody. Divide into groups of four and go. Each group should be separate from but in sight of a group at either side; that way we'll be pretty sure of covering all the ground." The husky young man who was speaking promptly gathered three more around him and led the way into the woods.

Peter looked at Kate. "Shall we?" he asked, nodding toward the band of searchers making for the trees.

"Let's," said Kate. "I'm crazy about the woods. During the school year we have a club—the Woodland Trail Club—which arranges for an all-day woods hike whenever the weather permits."

"Keep some of the others in sight," Peter cautioned. "We don't want to get lost."

"I couldn't get lost in these woods," laughed Kate. "I've been in them in all seasons."

They had to hurry to catch up with the nearest group, and like the others, they beat the bushes with long sticks they picked up and repeatedly called Herbie's name. The going was rough, and Kate stumbled more than once and was kept from falling only by Peter's steadying hand. It was hot in the woods—sweltering, in fact—and between the heat and the difficulty in trying to avoid the thorniest of the bushes, while keeping up a fast pace behind the others, Kate began to think she would have to ask Peter to stop and wait till the others made the return trip. At that moment there were three shots, which echoed through the woods loudly.

"Herbie's found!" cried Peter. "I heard them arranging to fire a shotgun three times in the air when the boy was located."

"Thanks be," said Kate. "I was just about to drop in my tracks. Could we sit down a minute by that brook I can hear giggling and gurgling, while I get my breath and cool off?"

There wasn't much water in the brook at that time of year, for they were in the midst of a hot dry spell. But at least there was some water, and as Kate pointed out, it was low enough to afford them a clear view of the pebbles and small stones at the bottom. She stooped and picked up a round white one. Peter found one studded with garnets.

"Jewels for your crown, my lady," he said, giving it to Kate.

"I'll keep it always to remind me of today," she told him, and though she was laughing, there was an undercurrent of seriousness in her tone.

"Don't make rash promises," Peter said lightly. "You'll be getting real jewels one of these days—a diamond ring, for instance, on *that* finger." He touched her ring finger, and Kate colored. Was this his way of leading up to a proposal? But Peter said no more about jewels. He was listening to the song of a bird in a tree overhead.

"I always wanted to be a bird-watcher," he said dreamily. "Imagine being able to sit like this in the woods, day after day, and learning to identify the songs of birds. You're a native of these parts, Kate; can you tell me what kind of bird is serenading us?"

"Probably a red-eyed vireo," said Kate a little snappishly. Why couldn't the man say what he meant—if he meant to ask her to marry him?

Peter did not appear to notice her annoyance. "Really?" he said. "What does the bird look like? And why are its eyes red?"

"I really haven't the least idea what it looks or sounds like or even if it is seen around here.

As for the red eyes, perhaps the bird needs glasses."

Peter threw back his head and laughed heartily. "I didn't know you had such a sense of humor, Kate. For a minute you had me fooled—I thought you really knew something about birds."

She wanted him to be very, very serious, very romantic, and she had put him in a hilarious mood. Kate stared at the pebbles in the bottom of the brook and wondered how she could bring the conversation around to more personal matters.

But before she could decide on a method of attack, there was a loud halloo from behind them, and Henry Johnson and three other members of the stage group arrived.

"News flash!" shouted Henry. "The kid's found. Didn't you hear the gun?"

"We heard," said Peter. "I take it he was all in one piece?"

"We hope, we hope," said Henry. "But we don't know. We didn't say we found him, you know. We only said he was found, and you said you knew that already. You ready to shove off now?"

"No," said Kate. "I dropped down here because if I had tried to take another step, I would have dropped dead. It was a near thing."

"Well, want us to wait?" said one of Henry's crowd, a youth whose sunburned nose was peeling.

"Shaddup, you social misfit," said Henry out of the corner of his mouth, in a whisper which was, however, perfectly audible to Peter and Kate.

"Okay, Freckles," said the other boy. "Go, man, go!" He waved farewell to Peter and Kate and plunged off into the underbrush. Henry and the others followed.

"We'll have to be going soon, at that," sighed Kate, turning to Peter. She began feeling around with one foot for her shoes, which she had kicked off when they first sat down. She found one, but the other seemed to have disappeared.

"I'll track it down," offered Peter. "Have you ever noticed that when you kick your shoes off, at least one of them walks away by itself and hides? Sneaky things, shoes."

He finally located the missing shoe under a fallen log and gallantly bent down to put it on Kate's foot. She moaned slightly.

"My foot has grown since we sat down," she observed. "Just this one—the other is still the right size. Now, I'll give it the old school try."

With Peter's help she got to her feet.

"Now then," said Peter, "front and center!"

As they made circuitous detours around heavy thickets and other uninviting woodland obstacles, Peter and Kate began to wonder if they were going in the right direction.

"We should have told the boys to leave a trail —bits of torn paper or broken twigs or something."

"I thought I had a general idea of the direction we took when we came into the maze," said Kate, "but I'm getting horribly afraid we're lost."

They plodded on. The sun clouded over, and shortly afterward it disappeared entirely.

"Not that it was doing us much good as a direction finder," said Peter. "After a few turns we couldn't tell anything from its position. Of course, if it had been setting—"

They found their way blocked by an enormous fallen tree, upended by some ancient storm, lying on its side. Its roots stood pathetically useless, turned beseechingly skyward, and its branches were entangled with errant berry bushes and young saplings. Without speaking, Kate and Peter climbed to the top of the mighty trunk and, joining hands, jumped together to the ground.

But it was not solid earth they struck. The huge crater left by the tree's torn roots had loosened the surrounding ground, and apparently an underground stream had continued the insidious work of destruction. Peter and Kate felt the earth give way beneath them as they jumped. They scrambled desperately for a foothold but only succeeded in loosening a widening area as they slid down, down, with the avalanche that was carrying them deep into the earth gaining force with every second. When they finally found themselves on solid ground, they discovered that only a small hole at the top of the cascade of earth and rocks left a patch of sky visible.

Chapter 9

Kate and Peter continued to sit flat on the packed earth, as they had landed, for a few minutes while they got back the breath that had been knocked out of them. They looked at each other in consternation. The silence had a queer, dead feeling as if they had dropped into another world. There was a faint smell compounded of damp earth and gas as if from a hole long closed up. At last Peter spoke.

"Have you any idea where we are?"

"I'm afraid I have. There used to be an old mine around here; they dug emery, I believe. But it's been closed down for many, many years, and I haven't the foggiest idea where it was located."

"That's just dandy." Peter made an attempt to get quickly to his feet and discovered he had sent more gravel pouring down on them. The next time he proceeded more cautiously and, by bending over, managed to keep from hitting the overhanging rock. He pulled Kate up to stand beside him.

"If this is the way the men entered the mine," Kate said tentatively, "I should think there would be a ramp or steps or something."

"It is my opinion that this was just an airshaft," Peter said. "There seems to be a passage leading straight ahead. Are you willing to risk going along it?"

Kate agreed in a small voice. She felt responsible for their predicament in a way, although it had not been her fault they had found the abandoned mine so unexpectedly.

Peter felt in his pocket for matches but could find only a small lighter. With its tiny glow, this enabled them to distinguish a steep path leading down into blackness and menacing rocks on either side. For the first time Kate was really frightened.

As if he sensed her reaction, Peter reached out and took her hand. Instinctively Kate shuffled her feet, bracing herself against the sharp descent. The narrow path seemed to lead nowhere but into blackness, and she found that she was breathing in small gasps. Involuntarily she looked back over her shoulder; the hole they had fallen through and the patch of sky above it seemed to have dwindled to almost nothing. She turned back to say something to Peter, and at that moment the lighter went out.

"Oh!" Kate could not repress an exclamation of dismay. Peter let go of her hand and worked with frantic fury to start the lighter again. For a few seconds it seemed as though it would not light. Then suddenly the flame shot up, and Kate thought she had never seen a more welcome sight in all her life.

"The air is probably bad in here after being shut up so long," Peter explained. "I'll be surprised if we don't start an explosion," he added.

"Don't be so cheerful," Kate snapped at him. "It's bad enough to be lost in this smelly old mine without having you suggest we'll be buried alive." In her annoyance Kate spoke in her usual voice, and Peter answered also in his natural tone.

"If you're going to go hysterical on me, I'll

leave you here and go ahead alone."

"You will *not* leave me here alone!" For emphasis Kate stamped her foot. "Maybe you think it's my fault—"

At that moment it happened. A little ahead of them there was a warning rumble and then the sharp sound of rocks falling from the sides and above. Now Peter did take her in his arms, but Kate had never felt less romantic in her life. It was perhaps only a second or two that the noise of falling rocks continued, and when at last it subsided Peter, without words, urged her back along the way they had come. The lighter had gone out again, but this time Peter was able to get it going without difficulty. They retraced their steps in silence, and Kate was surprised to find that they had progressed only a short distance from their original tiny haven of hard-packed earth.

Kate sat down slowly, and Peter sank onto the earth beside her. His shoulder touched hers, and she was surprised to find that he was trembling. He snapped off the lighter, and after a moment Kate was able to distinguish his features.

"Better save the fuel," he said apologetically.

"I don't expect we will be here very long, but it's just as well to keep what little light we have."

"You're right," Kate agreed, feeling as if a weight had been lifted from her chest. "It must be getting late in the afternoon, and Henry Johnson and the others know where we were at one point, anyway. What time is it, by the way?"

Peter lit the lighter again and glanced at the face of his watch. "I would forget to wind it," he said bitterly. "It stopped at half past two."

"I think it must be after four," Kate said, although she was not at all certain. "Perhaps by now they are already fanning out looking for us, the way we all did when Herbie was lost. If we just stay here—"

There was a sound like that of a distant shot, and Kate was about to remark that they were already found. But Peter was shaking his head gloomily.

"Don't get your hopes up," he cautioned her. "That sounded like a clap of thunder. The day has been so hot and humid we are surely due for a storm. Nobody will come looking for us if it is a real thunder and lightning affair. Too dangerous."

"It's lucky we are in the mine, then," Kate said, determined to be cheerful. "At least we won't get wet."

Peter's answer was continued silence, and for a while they sat side by side listening to the muted sound of a furious storm above. At one point Kate thought she could detect a splintering sound as if lightning had struck a nearby tree. But it might be only her imagination, she realized, because the patch of sky overhead that was now so dark had been briefly illumined. Peter continued to sit in silence.

"Don't worry so," Kate said at last. "I don't remember anyone being lost in the woods in the whole history of Clyde's Gap. There's always someone who has a vague idea where the missing party has gone, and the men form a sort of posse and keep searching all night, if necessary. The women generally set up a place where they can give out hot coffee and sandwiches. Gosh, I'm hungry!"

"We should have bought two box lunches apiece while we were at it." Peter still sounded quite desperate, but Kate was glad that he had at least spoken to her. Without pausing to think, she chattered on, gradually leaving the subject of those who had been lost to speak of the local life, humdrum as it might be. She mentioned several persons, including Farmer Reynolds, whose lives might form the basis of a plot for one of his plays.

At Peter's exclamation of disbelief, Kate went on to assure him that Jim Reynolds had not always been the plodding farmer that he now appeared. On the contrary, he had been considered rather "wild" by the elders of his generation and had been responsible for more than one escapade which were referred to only indirectly when Kate was around.

"If you want themes for your plots," Kate insisted, "you could not do better than to come to a small town like Clyde's Gap. We have many of the same problems that you have in a big city, but we are able to look at them more closely, as if we were using a microscope or something."

"But you have a quality of kindliness in a small town that you don't often find in a big city," Peter objected. "For instance, I understand Bob Morehouse left town under a cloud. But when the facts are known the whole incident is forgotten. Bob Morehouse returns to Clyde's Gap and—who knows?—may one day be its most honored citizen."

Kate pressed her advantage and continued to talk about the townspeople and their life, always in relation to the theatre and possible future dramatization. Afterward, she could not recall exactly what she had said. She knew only that Peter was responding more and more to her ideas and was even contributing a few of his own. When he finally began to talk of his own early life as the pampered son of a hard-headed manufacturer, Kate relaxed. She was suddenly very tired and would have liked nothing better than to close her eyes and resign herself to whatever fate might have in store. But she forced herself to keep making appropriate comments so that Peter would keep talking. So intent was she upon maintaining this attitude that she almost missed hearing her name called in the distance again and again, in a faint voice. Involuntarily she put her hand on Peter's arm to silence him, and they listened together.

"Kate! Kate Scott! Kate, where are you?"

Peter jumped to his feet, heedless now of

the trickle of gravel that poured down at his movement.

"Here we are!" he shouted. "We're both here in this old mine! Over here by that big tree that's fallen down. Help, whoever you are! Get us out of here!"

It seemed like a long time, but Kate realized later that it must have been only a few moments before Gil's face was peering down at them from above. His bulky shoulders shut out what little light there was, and Kate almost sobbed as she realized that the horrible experience was nearly over. Peter was explaining how they had happened to be in such a predicament and how they had been afraid to try to climb back up the way they had come for fear they would close up the hole entirely.

"Why did it take you so long to find us?" he asked. "We've been here for hours and hours."

"We've been looking for you exactly an hour and forty-five minutes," Gill retorted. "In case you don't know it, there was quite a thunderstorm up here. Trees crashing all over the place. Somebody might have been killed."

"I wonder you bothered to keep searching," Peter said sarcastically.

"We wouldn't have bothered on your account," Gil said in the same vein, "but we figured you had Kate Scott with you, and she's one of our gang."

"Cut the chatter and get us out of here," Peter demanded. "I don't suppose you had sense enough to bring along a piece of rope."

"It will take more than a piece of rope to get you out of there," Gil rejoined. "In my opinion, you will need something like a derrick. But hold on. I'll round up the others and we'll figure out some way. You okay, Kate?"

"I am perfectly all right," Kate managed to say. And then, without warning, she burst into tears. She tried to add the word, "Hurry!" but found she could say nothing at all.

The next interval was blurred. Kate had a vague impression that Peter kept urging her not to cry and that she kept sobbing for a long time in spite of his efforts. How much later it was she did not know, but eventually a noose was lowered through the opening above and Peter instructed her to sit in it and hold on tightly. She remembered striking against the sides of the slide as she was being pulled up by strong hands. There was the sudden breath of fresh air, cool and damp, that set her shivering. Then she was lying on a blanket on the ground and listening to the sounds of Peter's rescue as if from a great distance.

Later she was told that the "strong hands" that had pulled on the rope were in reality a winch that had been hastily commandeered from a nearby farm. The mechanism was usually attached to a tractor and was used for hauling grain into a silo, but it had worked equally well in raising Kate and Peter to ground level.

When the excitement died down the play again assumed its place in the spotlight of summer activities. Peter called a special meeting of the various committees dealing with properties for the stage, the sale of tickets, the wardrobe requirements and the publicity. He was especially dissatisfied with the efforts of the publicity committee and the resulting slow sale of tickets.

"But the play won't go on for a long time yet," the chairman of the committee insisted. "There's lots of time to sell tickets."

That was not the right attitude to take, Peter told the sulky young man standing before him. For many professional performances, tickets were sold as much as six months or a year ahead of time, and even so there had to be a strong effort made just before the show went on. It was his idea, Peter went on, to capitalize on the small news item that had been written about Kate when she had been rescued from the abandoned mine. He proposed that the juvenile lead, accompanied by a member of the publicity committee, go around to the summer hotels and boarding houses and talk up the community project that was being put on by the young people of Clyde's Gap.

This idea was promptly accepted by the members of the publicity committee, who at once gave Kate her special assignment, to take off that very afternoon for the Berkshire Chalet.

"You'd better go home and dress first," Peter said, looking critically at Kate's working costume of white shorts and striped pullover. "Also, take along several pairs of tickets and present them to the manager of the hotel with the compliments of the cast. As a matter of fact, you ought to

allow for at least five pairs of free tickets for
every performance."

"Gee, why?" asked the publicity chairman.
"I thought the whole idea of this business was
to make some money."

"You'll make more money, because you'll sell
more tickets if you do as I say," Peter said stern-
ly. "Now scoot, the two of you. The rest of us
will go on with the rehearsal and concentrate on
those scenes where Kate does not appear."

Kate was glad she had the pink handkerchief
linen dress fresh and ready to wear. She brushed
her fair hair until it shone but decided against
putting it on top of her head. Instead she fluffed
it out over the ears and attached a small pink
bow at one side. The chairman of the publicity
committee whistled when he saw her and proudly
escorted Kate to a sleek and shining roadster. It
was borrowed from a friend of his, he explained.
Although he had not thought to change from his
own rumpled slacks and sweatshirt and offered
to stay in the car, Kate insisted that he should
come in with her when they stopped at the Berkshire Chalet.

Her heart gave a little throb as they drew up

before the spot that had so far been the glamorous highlight of the summer for her. Without Peter beside her she felt very young and unsure of herself. The Chalet, too, looked different in broad daylight from the way it had looked on that very special night. For all the laughter and gayety of the guests around the swimming pool and on the tennis courts, there was a businesslike air about the hostelry.

Perhaps, Kate thought, as she walked across the patio, it wasn't only the moonlight and the fact that I was coming here for the first time that made it seem different. Perhaps when you're with the one man who really counts you see things from a different point of view. I know I'll treasure the memory of that night forever.

Chapter 10

There were difficulties in getting the rehearsals started in earnest on the day Peter Howard felt they should "be putting the show on the road." In the first place, the stage crew had not quite finished building its platform and there was still hammering and talking among the workers.

"Can't we have some quiet around here?" Peter demanded of Kate.

She had noticed that Peter had become increasingly short-tempered since the night they had seen Martina at the Berkshire Chalet. Kate was getting a little short-tempered herself and was inclined to be unsympathetic.

"If you're putting on a play you have to have a stage to work on," she said sharply.

"Well, we can't work on it while its in the

process of construction, that's for sure."

"Perhaps we could go outside and use some tree stumps or stones as props."

"We'll have to do something," Peter said ungraciously. "I suppose that's as good an idea as any."

"And where's Martina?" he demanded. "Didn't she know I called a rehearsal for ten sharp this morning? It's already ten-thirty. Oh, she's coming now. I suppose we should be grateful that she shows up at all," he finished as her small coupé drove past the door.

"I don't think anyone will show up any more if your temper doesn't improve," Kate retorted, and was glad to see that she had at last made an impression.

"I guess I have been pretty hard to get along with," Peter admitted. "But I have the good excuse of being the playwright as well as the director and coach. And what with all this hammering and talking—" He broke off as he saw Kate's stormy glance, and said instead, "Let's go outside."

Kate wondered for a minute if Peter thought she had taken too much on herself in rebuking him. However, he did seem to make an attempt to be more agreeable and, oddly enough, he did not even say anything to Martina about being late.

Kate, as the first one on the stage when the play opened, was supposed to be at the door of the room as Bob Morehouse, Henry Johnson and Stella Rand came in. The scene was concerned only with the teen-agers, and both Kate and Stella found it an easy scene to do. Kate, in particular, drew a word of praise from Peter.

"That's it," he told her. "You are supposed to be among friends you have known all your life. You're gay and light-hearted, but you do show that you are fond of Bob Morehouse and that you expect you will be engaged when you graduate from school. You might well overdraw the character slightly, because you have to contrast this scene with one in the second act.

"Wait a minute. Maybe we should have music. You can put a record-roll on the player piano."

"A player piano?"

"Or one of those old-fashioned morning glories that they used before record players came along," he said impatiently. "We'll iron that out later, when we see what the furniture committee can dig up at the farms around here."

"Sure, let's live it up!" Bob Morehouse exclaimed, grabbing Kate around the middle and whirling her off into a fast step while he hummed a rhumba tune.

"Not so fast," Peter objected. "This is way back—remember? No rock and roll; no twist."

For answer Bob held Kate at arm's length and waltzed her slowly around the grass. Stella and Henry were so convulsed with laughter that they could hardly contain themselves, and even Peter had to smile. Kate in blue jeans and sneakers and Bob Morehouse in shorts and a T-shirt did not make a very old-fashioned-looking couple.

"What's going on here?" Jim Reynolds asked, walking across the road.

"We're rehearsing," Peter said. "But you don't come on stage for a while yet, so you've got time to feed the chickens or pitch hay if you want to."

"Hallie said she'd do the chores," the farmer assured them. "I'll just sit here and watch.

"You would," Peter muttered under his breath, but Reynolds had already found a convenient tree stump and settled down. As Peter had suspected, he was not above interrupting the players in order to get his own bit part more clearly in mind.

"Am I supposed to be Bob's father?" he demanded. "And I'm supposed to be a farmer, too? Is that it?"

"Yes, that's right," Peter said, irritated. "It's getting on toward evening, and you've just finished the farm chores, when you come on. All right, Kate—better take that line over again."

"No farmer worthy of his salt would let a big, husky fellow like Bob get out of doing half the chores while he went into the parlor and danced," Jim Reynolds pointed out dryly. Peter seemed to be about to give up the whole idea of rehearsing the first scene.

"All right, gang; we'll skip the next lines and take it from where Mr. Reynolds comes in. When you come into the scene, Jim, you disapprove of the youngsters and look at them so blackly that they immediately make an excuse to leave you and Bob alone.

"Bob will ask you if you've finished up down in the barn. You look at him for a long time before answering. And then you just say: 'Nope.' "

"I'd say more than that," Farmer Reynolds interrupted, bluntly. "There's a lot to do around a barn, come nighttime, and I wouldn't stand for no youngster of mine leavin' me with all the heavy work to do."

Kate thought that Peter was about to explode and saw that Miss Dawson was also worried about the playwright's reaction to the farmer's advice. It was at this providential moment that Hallie's clarion voice was raised in a strident shout.

"You, Jim Reynolds, come back over here! The Jersey cow got loose again, and she'll be wandering out on the road, next thing you know."

"That's all right," Peter said with evident relief. "We can rehearse you some other time." As the farmer disappeared, he took out a large handkerchief and mopped his face. "One more interruption," he said, "and I'll go back to the peace and quiet of New York."

From then on, Peter made them really work, and Stella, who had forgotten her lines, was reduced almost to tears by his sarcastic comments on the way she was rewriting his play. Even Kate came in for some criticism.

"You've just lost your boy friend to a glamorous movie star," he told her. "It isn't quite the end of the world, but you think it is. This is the scene I told you about that is a sharp contrast to the first scene, where you were so gay and light-hearted. You've got to grow up a little, Kate."

She tried, but Peter had her do the scene over and over again until she was ready to drop. However, he did not seem satisfied with her last version any more than he had been the first time she went through her lines. But he finally did allow her to make her exit, although he was shaking his head as she walked off the stage.

The only break Peter Howard gave the cast was a half-hour to eat the lunch each had brought. Stella was getting a little tired of the whole idea. Kate could sympathize with her, because she did have a comparatively minor role and it cut down her chances of talking alone with Bob Morehouse. He, on the contrary, was on the stage almost every minute during the play, and so her chances for a private tête-à-tête now and then were practically zero.

It seemed to Kate that Stella's red hair was a flaming banner when they started back for rehearsals.

"I don't know why Peter has to keep us all hanging around when he spends so much time coaching just Bob and Miss Dawson," Stella muttered.

"After all, they are the leading characters," Kate said gently, "and if you're really interested in the theatre I should think you'd enjoy watching other people rehearse."

"Well, I don't," Stella said flatly. "If we don't get a little excitement around here, I'm going to flip. I really am. As for making a career for myself on the stage, what chance is there for anyone who's nicknamed Fatso?"

Peter called Kate at just that moment, and she had a brief scene alone with Bob before Miss Dawson, as an aging movie queen, came back onto the set. It was this scene that Peter kept insisting should be played as a dramatic role. But Kate didn't feel in the least dramatic. Ever since Peter had praised her that morning she had been almost deliriously happy.

"Say, Bob," Peter said, just before Kate finished the scene, "I haven't seen your brother around all day."

"He said he'd stop by later. Are you worried for fear he's been hired by some talent scout?"

"No." Peter grinned. "But I understand he's on the furniture committee, and I thought he could round up a player piano for us."

"I know where they have one," Bob said unexpectedly. "It's right across the road there in Jim Reynolds' parlor. I saw it when I was around the place so much fixing the tractor."

"Good," said Peter. "But I'd still like to see your brother when he gets here. I wouldn't want to interfere with the furniture committee," he explained.

Kate thought it rather odd that Peter should make such a point of seeing Gil. But since it would give her a few minutes extra with Peter—maybe a story conference—she didn't bother much about the reason for his request.

It lacked a few minutes of five when Peter glanced at his watch and dismissed the cast for the day. Then he went inside the barn and told the workers that they could knock off, too. Kate watched Stella and Bob drive off. It was plain to see that Stella had been thoroughly bored by the time the day ended. Yet Martina Dawson, who had the largest part, next to Bob Morehouse, and who had been rehearsing almost constantly, seemed fresh and sparkling as she got into her car.

Finally everyone else was gone, and Kate was left alone with Peter.

"Well, Kate, did you want to see me about something?" he asked.

"It's that second scene," Kate began; "you know, the one where I'm supposed to be so sad—"

"It would help you to think of something sad," Peter explained. "It needn't have anything to do with the play. You didn't get an invitation to that big fraternity dance, and you'd already bought your dress, for instance."

For answer Kate smiled at him. "It would be hard to imagine something like that. In fact, the saddest thing that's happened to me so far was flunking a geometry exam, and even that I was allowed to take over again the following year."

Peter seemed not particularly interested in her

problem. He stood looking at her in a cool, impersonal way that Kate found disconcerting. When she could stand it no longer, she burst out:

"I'm sorry if I'm disturbing your line of thought. Anyway, there's Gil coming in right now; you probably want to talk to him alone."

"No, you can stay if you want to." Peter's glance was still impersonal, and Kate had the impression he was not even seeing her. She had noticed before that he had a quality of concentration that cut out everything but his work of the moment. As Gil came toward them he greeted Peter casually and said, "Hi, Kate! I stopped by to see if you needed a ride home."

"Then you didn't get my message? I particularly wanted to see you tonight, Gil," said Peter.

"It's about a player piano—" Kate began.

"No, it isn't about a player piano," Peter contradicted. "It's about Gil's singing. I heard you doing an aria from 'Lucia.' First you sang it in the traditional way; but when you got here to the barn you started swinging it."

"Oh, that." Gil's voice was disparaging. "I do that just to amuse myself—and annoy the neighbors. Some real music lovers around here."

"Do you know any other familiar arias?" Peter asked.

"Oh yes, Gil, do the one from 'Figaro,' " Kate urged him. "I think I like that one best."

"You mean you want me to do it right *now*?" Gil said with patent disbelief. "Why should I? You lookin' for laughs?"

"Never mind what I'm looking for," Peter said sharply. "Say you're doing it just to amuse Kate and myself."

Gil, looking startled at the way the director grouped himself with Kate, stepped to one side. "Okay," he said, "but I still think it's some kind of a gag."

Without further preliminary he opened his mouth, murmured, "Mi, mi, mi," then launched into the aria from "Figaro." After a few soulful notes he snapped his fingers, did a funny little shuffling step that was reminiscent of calypso dancers and "swung" into the middle of the aria —literally.

Kate clapped her hands as he broke off suddenly.

"I wanna know what this is all about," Gil said.

"Sure," said Peter. "I just had to find out if you did as well as I thought you did, my boy. You're okay, laddie. I want to spot you in the intermission between the acts. You may not know it, but there are just two acts to the play, and I think a couple of arias by you would go over well with the audience."

"Aw, I couldn't do that," Gil said. "My gang would think it a hoot—my standin' up there and makin' like an opera star."

"Oh, but, Gil, you must," Kate insisted. "After all, Mr. Howard knows what he wants and what audiences like. If he thinks your songs will add to the entertainment of the evening, I think you ought to cooperate."

Gil looked at her for a moment without answering. Then he shrugged: "Okay, it's your ears. But remember, everybody has heard me for miles around while I was delivering papers, and they won't think it much of a treat to pay hard cash to hear me howl."

"You let me be the judge of that," Peter said firmly. "As a matter of fact, not only have the people for miles around heard you, but I'm planning on bringing some people from New

York to see the play and they'll be hearing you at the same time."

"You talked me into this, Kate." Gil groaned. "But I don't hold it against you. I'll give you a lift."

"Thanks," said Kate weakly. She threw an imploring look at Peter. But he wasn't looking at her. She was grateful for Gil's attention, in view of Peter's lack of interest, and when he asked her to go for a ride with him after dinner she accepted.

Chapter 11

The evening was very warm and the scent of the pines all around them was very strong.

"Smells like one of those pine-flavored deodorants they spray around in the air, doesn't it?" said Gil Morehouse, after he had killed the engine of his car and was leaning back in the seat.

"A romantic comparison." Kate Scott turned in her seat to stare at Gil. He seemed tense, as if waiting for something to happen. They were parked in a narrow overgrown lane that led off the main road, hard-surfaced but seldom used, since the state highway that paralleled it had been completed some months before.

Was Gil trying to get up courage enough to kiss her? Kate wondered as the minutes passed. He wasn't even trying to put an arm around her shoulders or to take her hand. His own hands were resting on the wheel; clutching it, in fact.

"Expecting someone?" she asked, after another minute of heavy silence.

"What?" said Gil, as if startled.

"You returning from orbit?" Kate was becoming irritated. "I asked if you were expecting someone."

"I had a special reason for asking you to come out here tonight," said Gil. "You're a friend of Stella Rand's, aren't you?"

"You know I am," said Kate. "What about her?"

"I thought somebody who was a friend of hers ought to be here in case—in case—"

"What's the matter with you, Gil? What is this all about, and where's Stella?"

"Maybe I should have told you before. Bob has Stella in his car, and he and Blair Williams— you know Blair Williams, don't you?"

"I know who he is. His family has a summer place up there in the hills—a big place called The Lodge."

"That's the guy. Well, he and Bob had a run-in the other night; something about Bob's cutting the Williams fellow's car off when they were leaving a parking space. They got into an argument and this Blair Williams dared Bob to settle it with a chicken race."

"Bob didn't—?"

"You know Bob. He'd never refuse to take a dare. They set a date for the race—tonight. Here."

"Bob's a hot rodder, but—a chicken race! You mean those two nuts are going to aim their cars at each other, coming from different directions? It's like fighting a duel, only worse."

"It's dangerous, all right," said Gil. "To make it worse, Bob's got Stella in his car. She wouldn't let him go without her. This Williams fellow has a girl with him, too; I don't know who she is. Williams isn't in our crowd, of course."

"Why didn't you tell me this before bringing me out here?" demanded Kate angrily. "I would have told Stella's father. Maybe there's still time, if we could get to a telephone."

"It's too late. Anyway, Stella and Bob would both be furious if you blabbed to Stella's old man. And you'd lose every friend you've got. Nobody'd trust a snitcher."

"I don't care! This is a matter of life and death. They may all be killed, or hurt terribly. I don't understand you, Gil, not lifting a finger to save them! You're a—what do they call it?— a sadist. You enjoy seeing people suffer. But I won't sit still and see anything like this happen to Stella. Start the car. Get going. We've got to find them before this crazy race begins!"

"We'd be caught in the middle if we went out there now."

"All right, if you won't drive me I'll run down the road waving something—my white sweater." Kate opened the door on her side and jumped out.

"Come back here, you little idiot!" Gil leaped over the door beside him and ran to seize Kate by the arm. "Listen—there's the signal."

The blast of a distant horn came clearly over the still air. In spite of herself Kate stood rooted to the spot, rigid. The blast was repeated a second time, then a third, in quick succession. From the other direction came another blast of a horn, also repeated a second and third time. It was a signal—there was no mistake about that. Kate climbed back into the car.

"I hate you, Gil Morehouse." She spoke through chattering teeth. She had begun to shudder violently. Her words still hung on the air as she heard the rush of tires along the road, coming from both directions. Then Bob's car streaked past. Now—she strained her eyes and ears—the crash must come, unless Bob or Blair Williams turned chicken. But instead of a crash, there was a girl's scream, high and piercing, and a sound she could not identify. Gil swung his car onto the road with such a jolt that she had to catch hold of the door to keep from falling.

"There they are!" Gil maneuvered his car slightly off the road, at a point where Bob's car was motionless. Just beyond it, in the ditch on the opposite side, the other car was upside down, its wheels still spinning in the air. There was a spurt of flame, and silhouetted against the light Kate could see dark running figures, two running away from the overturned car; the other—Bob—running toward it.

"Bob! Bob! Come back!" That was Stella's voice, coming from Bob's car, in an hysterical wail. She wasn't hurt, then.

Bob had now met the two running figures, and

Kate was so intent upon them that for an instant she didn't realize that Gil had jumped from the seat beside her and was racing toward the others. Then she saw him seize one of the figures—the girl—as Bob caught her by the other arm and together, with the girl propelled between them, they made unbelievable speed toward Gil's car. An explosion seemed to tear the air apart. Flames shot higher, outlining the wheels of the Williams car, still turning helplessly. There was another explosion, a bigger one, and as the running figures came alongside the car where she was sitting horrified, the Williams car was entirely enveloped in flames.

Blair's girl clung to the door beside Kate and turned to look at the blazing ruin farther up the road.

"You all right?" Bob asked briefly. The girl nodded. Bob ran to his own car where Stella was still shrieking, apparently unable to stop.

Blair Williams, who had said nothing at all up to that moment, now made one comment. "Whew!" he said.

"Yeah," echoed Gil. "Whew!"

In the distance they could hear the sound of

a state police car siren.

"Cops!" said Blair Williams. "The works. Wait till Dad gets the bad news. He'll blow his top."

"Will they arrest us?" asked the girl. "My mother won't like it if I have to go to jail."

"That sounds like an understatement to me, from what I've seen of your mother," observed Blair. "Now, all of you keep your trap shut about the race. This was just an accident that could happen to anybody."

Then the first police car hurtled to a stop. An ambulance was following soon and another police car. Stella was still crying in that weird, high way as the state policemen started asking questions. The doctor who had jumped out of the ambulance ran to Bob's car. In a moment, Stella's screams stopped.

None of it seemed real to Kate.

Rehearsals had been going along swimmingly, but they had to be called off the day all concerned in the chicken race had to appear in adolescents' court. Kate and Gil were called as witnesses. Everybody had tried desperately, the night of the disastrous race, to conceal the fact that a chicken race had been in progress, but the state police were astute and got the story, bit by bit. Blair Williams had not turned chicken. His car had simply left the road when it hit a curve and, traveling at a speed that would not have been sneered at by a racing car enthusiast, had, as Williams expressed it in court," sort of become air-borne."

It turned out that the sleek truck Blair Williams was driving had been one of the new pick-up jobs. Blair told the court proudly that it had an unique grind on the cam shaft.

"Steps up the horsepower," he explained happily. Then he remembered. His car was a total loss. He looked appealingly at his father—all the participants were accompanied at official request, by parents or guardians—and received such a black look that his own face clouded. The chances for getting another such car appeared very slim at the moment.

It was a subdued group who finally left the courthouse. Stella's father had her firmly by the arm. Bob Morehouse attempted to speak to her, but was waved aside by the embattled Mr. Rand.

Kate, not noticing the storm signals in her absorption over the stinging lecture the judge had given them, spoke to Stella as she passed.

"Rehearsal at ten tomorrow as usual," she said.

"Stella will not be at rehearsal tomorrow or any other day," Mr. Rand said fiercely, scowling at Kate, who fell back a few paces.

"But what will we do?" she asked Gil. "Stella is an important member of the cast."

"She can be replaced," said Gil largely. "Anyone can be replaced. I'm sure glad, though, all the money Stella's old man gave us has been spent already. He would prabably make us give it back."

They walked on awhile in silence.

"You don't really hate me, do you, Kate?" Gil burst out finally.

Kate was genuinely surprised. "What makes you think I hate you?" she demanded.

"You said so—you know, when we were out there on the road and you were mad because I hadn't let you know about the chicken race in time to warn Stella's father."

"Oh, that," said Kate. "I just lost my head

when I thought that Bob and Stella were likely to be killed or hurt. I guess I could never hate you, Gil. We've been friends so long."

"I wish we could go steady," sighed Gil.

"You know we've had that out before," said Kate. "Mom doesn't approve of going steady. She says teenagers should be growing up, not trying to take on adult responsibilities—as they may have to do if the going steady leads to teen-age marriage."

"But you're practically going steady with me," Gil pointed out. "All last year we dated for basketball games and dances."

"I know, but Mom didn't like it. She says next year I've got to date different boys. Maybe there won't be any next year at Clyde's Gap High. Maybe I'll be in New York, on the stage."

"Gee," said Gil. "What do you want to go and do that for?"

Kate didn't answer. She had a sudden vision of Peter Howard telling her: "A girl with your talent for the stage is wasting her life in Clyde's Gap. You're young, of course, but not too young to start your career. Some of the current stars started at fourteen or even younger. And remember, I'll be right there to help you over the rough places."

She sighed. It was only a dream as yet. But she would make it come true! She would make even more of an effort to impress Peter Howard with her ability. He was, she was sure, a little bit in love with her already, but it wasn't just love she wanted. She wanted a stage career. Love and marriage could wait, unless Peter was too insistent. Then, naturally, she would combine both.

When Peter Howard confronted the cast the next morning he found a dejected group.

"Look alive, you lads and lassies," he commanded. "Everybody here?" He looked around the group. "Hey, where's our red-headed Fatso?"

It's mean of him to call her that, Kate thought to herself. Stella isn't all *that* fat. If she wanted to starve herself like these Hollywood actresses— She felt unusually sympathetic with Stella after her father's pronouncement of yesterday.

"Stella Rand is out of the play, Mr. Howard," she said aloud. "Her father won't let her act in it, or even come to watch the rest of us."

Peter Howard stared at Kate, speechless for a moment. "It's too late to find a replacement," he said then. "Who would have thought we'd need understudies?" He looked from one gloomy fact to another.

"It's all the fault of that chicken race business, isn't it? You, Bob Morehouse, what were you thinking of—taking Stella with you on a stunt like that? Somebody might have been killed— even somebody tooling along the road who happened by when you were having your crazy race. Are you a congenital idiot, or what? You're older than these other kids, too; it's high time you showed some sense."

"Bob wasn't in this alone, Mr. Howard," Gil broke in. "I was there, watching the race. I knew about it beforehand. And Kate Scott was with me."

"Did she know about it before you went out there?"

"No," admitted Gil. "I didn't tell her till we were out on the road, waiting for the start of the race. Even then she tried to get me to telephone Stella's father—but it was too late."

Peter Howard looked at Kate, and his face softened. "Good girl," he said. "I'm glad to see one member of this cast has a head on her shoulders."

Kate colored furiously at the praise, but Bob, she saw, looked hostile.

"I know you kids love danger," Peter went on, "but life is dangerous enough in any case, without going out of your way to create danger. That's just foolishness. Even astronauts don't take dangerous chances. They study and train and take every possible precaution before they embark on a space ship.

"Even professional auto racers don't take crazy chances. They try to win the race, sure, but they don't get out on the track and try to run head on into each other. Wouldn't they look pretty ridiculous if they did?

"You kids who go in for chicken racing are being just as ridiculous as star racers would be to try a stunt like that. You proved nothing by taking a foolish dare. It just shows you're not very bright, that's all.

"Now, I'm here to put on a play and make a success of it. I can't do that if I don't have a well-trained cast. We've lost one member already; maybe we can make up for that. But if I hear of any more foolish chicken racing, or anything like it, I'll not only fire those who take part in it; I'll give up the play altogether and go back to New York."

He glared around the circle of serious faces as he spoke. But when his eye caught Martina Dawson's, he continued to stare at her for a moment. She stared back, then nodded slightly. She turned quietly and went toward her car.

Chapter 12

Banker Rand was red-haired, like his daughter
Stella. He rose and came from behind his desk
as Martina Dawson entered his cubicle. As he
often said, he did not believe in closed-door
offices for bank presidents. Let the public see
what was going on, and that the president of their
favorite bank was right out in plain view with
the rest of the staff, available to all comers. It
didn't quite work out that way, of course. Stray
callers knew better than to barge through the
low gate in the fence that set him somewhat
apart from the herd; there were guards to pre-
vent just that sort of thing. But it was vaguely
comforting to those who had money in Rand's
bank to see him sitting behind his desk, busy
with bank paper of one kind or another, without

any apparent immediate plans to rifle the vaults and run for it.

Now President Rand came forward to meet Martina, a benign smile on his golfer's brown face.

"Miss Dawson!" he exclaimed. "Delighted to see you, and to serve you, if I may?"

Martina took the chair he indicated and returned his smile.

"This is just a friendly visit," explained Martina. "No stocks, bonds or mortgages involved. I dropped in to have a little chat about Stella. She's in my English class at school, you know."

"Oh, indeed, I know that very well. Stella has unbounded admiration for you. She sings your praises from morning till night."

This somewhat exaggerated account of Stella's behavior gave Martina pause. It was more difficult than ever to introduce the topic she had come to discuss—Daddy Rand's ultimatum about Stella's participation in the play. Her bright color grew brighter as she fixed her eyes on the bank president's beaming face and plunged:

"Mr. Rand, you know of course that our young people are working hard to make a success of their theatrical production. They are doing it all on their own, with the assistance of the playwright-coach, Mr. Peter Howard, and some standby aid from myself. Stella has been doing splendidly in one of the most important roles."

Mr. Rand's smile had vanished. His brow had darkened; his red hair seemed to flame above his hot, angry eyes.

"I'm responsible for Stella's future, my dear Miss Dawson," he said. "It is my considered opinion that there may be very little future for a girl who thinks it fun to chicken race. That's what they call it, I believe."

"I'm just as set against hot-rodding and chicken racing as you are, Mr. Rand," said Stella. "But don't you see if something better is substituted, something like helping put on a community play, there won't be much time left over for dangerous stunts?"

"Stella made time to scour the countryside with a hot-rodder," said Mr. Rand, "in spite of her role in your play. Having to rehearse gave her an excuse to stay away from home for long periods as well as the opportunity to horse around with a no-good like Bob Morehouse."

"I think you do Bob Morehouse an injustice, Mr. Rand. He's daring, that's true, but maybe not too daring for the kind of world that will be in a couple of years. I understand he is something of a genius with machinery, so who can blame him if he pins his faith to motors and wheels? The day may come when he'll be in that group of daring young men on whom our own lives may depend—the technological experts on whom our position in the atomic world will surely rest."

"Let him fly as high as he likes—I'm not telling Bob Morehouse what to do with his life. What I'm saying is that I will no longer give him the opportunity to risk my daughter's life in one of his daredevil ventures."

"Your motive, Mr. Rand, I can well understand," said Martina, her face very serious. "But I think you are going the wrong way about it. Shutting Stella off from the community activities in which her friends are taking part will not keep her out of danger. Rather I think she will be driven to rebel to a degree you don't anticipate now. Stella is a high-spirited girl. She needs guidance, not constraint. You may force her into some terrible mistake, just to prove to herself—

and you—that in the everyday vernacular, she can take care of herself."

"I suppose you're suggesting that I may drive her into eloping with Bob."

"Isn't that a possibility?"

Mr. Rand took a folded linen handkerchief from his pocket and wiped his brow. "I wish Stella's mother were alive," he muttered. "It's no job for a man—trying to bring up a teen-aged daughter."

"I believe even mothers have many problems nowadays," smiled Martina. "There's no denying that our era presents extraordinary difficulties for both middle-aged and young. Teen-agers are children, not adults, but they are assuming in many cases the doubtful privileges and certainly the attitudes of older boys and girls."

"Have you any suggestion in Stella's case, beyond letting her run wild with Bob Morehouse?"

"I'm not suggesting anything of the sort," said Martina with spirit. "I think Bob Morehouse is a reasonable young man, who means well but, being a product of his time and place, is thoroughly in love with danger. However, if you had a talk with him and got him to promise to leave

Stella out of any future plans of his for dare-deviltry, he would abide by your rules. Incidentally, Peter Howard, the coach, has already warned the cast that any future escapade such as the chicken racing will result in his immediate departure for New York, and the play will be abandoned."

"And if I get such a promise from Bob, I'm supposed to let Stella return to the cast?"

"I think that would be wise," Martina advised him, "without, of course, saying anything to her about your pact with Bob."

"I suppose you're right," Mr. Rand agreed after a minute's reflection.

"I'm going back to the barn now. Have I your permission to announce that Stella will resume her role tomorrow?"

Mr. Rand nodded. "And while you're there, will you tell Bob Morehouse—he'll be around, I suppose—that I'd like to see him tonight at my house at eight o'clock for a friendly man-to-man chat about automobiles? I'm thinking of buying a new one, and I understand he's an expert in that line."

He grinned conspiratorially at Martina as she

rose to go.

"And I worried about the way you'd react to my interference," she murmured. "I should have known that bank presidents are diplomats at heart."

The next morning Martina Dawson arrived at the barn a little early. She was hoping she would find Peter already there, but although it was ten o'clock he had not yet arrived. The boys were still busy hammering in the barn, however, and Kate came around the corner just as Martina got out of the car.

"I guess we'll have to rehearse outside again today, Miss Dawson," Kate said apologetically. "I'm sure that Peter can't stand the hammering, and the boys are not quite finished."

"Don't you think Peter Howard should be the one to decide that?" Martina asked, looking at Kate sharply. "You know it is up to the coach and director to set the time and place for rehearsal. Peter has been lenient with us, but we must not tell him how to do his own work."

Kate could feel the color rising in her face. She sensed by Miss Dawson's tone that she was being told in a gentle way that she was assuming too much. "I didn't mean to be a big shot around here," Kate protested. "But Peter does consult me on a lot of things, and I thought—"

"It's all right," Martina agreed. "And I'm sure that Peter will call the rehearsal somewhere outside the barn. But I just wanted to warn you that stage directors—and playwrights as well— are on the temperamental side. After the upset we had last night over that chicken race, I'd like things to go as smoothly as possible for a change."

"But that's just it," Kate said with a worried frown. "With Stella out of the play, we'll have to find a new replacement, and I don't know of anyone who would be willing to take it on such short notice."

Martina Dawson did not answer, but a few minutes later when Peter had arrived she went over and spoke to him for a few minutes. Evidently it was an engrossing conversation, and Kate felt a twinge of jealousy as Peter suddenly grasped the teacher by the shoulders and hugged her hard. Kate had sensed that Peter and Martina had been quarreling the night Martina had appeared at the Berkshire Chalet with another escort. But there was no doubting, from the teacher's bright smile and Peter's enthusiastic hug, that the quarrel was definitely a thing of the past.

So they've made up, she thought to herself. I suppose it is better this way. But Peter will never forget that Miss Dawson turned him down for another man. He's probably just as conscientious as I am and wants to have the play go smoothly.

This was small comfort, but at least it helped console Kate for the moment. Gil Morehouse and his brother had arrived and assisted by Farmer Reynolds and two of the other boys, were hauling a player piano from the farm across the road. It was quite a big operation. To Kate's mind, the boys were doing all right and had the piano mounted on a trailer which was attached to the Farmer's tractor.

But Hallie Reynolds had suddenly developed a deep attachment for the relic and, although it had stood in one of the barns for years and was covered with dust, kept insisting that the boys be more careful as they handled it. Kate went over to assure the woman that they would take great care of this important prop and that it would be returned in apple-pie condition.

When Kate went back to the barn, Peter was inside approving of the latest carpentry work and suggesting an arrangement for the canvas flats that would form the background. She heard him speak to Bob Morehouse and ask him to stay after the others had gone.

"If it's about the chicken race," Kate said, "I think it is more important that we try to get a replacement for Stella than it is to do anything else." She blushed as she realized she was doing the very thing that Miss Dawson had cautioned her against.

"We don't have to worry about replacing Stella," Peter said, apparently not noticing her officiousness. "Martina has just told me that she saw Stella's father yesterday, and he agreed that Stella could return to the play."

"Oh!" Kate felt suddenly deflated. "I wonder why Miss Dawson didn't tell me when we were talking together."

"Perhaps because she felt the director should be the first to know," Peter said gently. "But anyway, you know now, and Stella is here."

The stage crew as well as the actors in the play converged on the car as it drove up to the barn. There was no mistaking the storm signals in Stella's eyes, and she made no move to get out of the car when it had stopped. Beside her, surprisingly, sat her father, Banker Rand, looking more serious that Kate had even seen him. Martina Dawson approached the car slowly, a questioning look on her face.

"Miss Dawson, I know I promised Stella might come back to the play today," the banker said heavily. "I have had to change that. Stella is furious about the whole matter; says she would like to go out west somewhere, like that Blair Williams who was also involved in the chicken race. His father has already sent him off to a dude ranch."

"But Stella can't do that," Peter protested. "Now that she's got your permission to go on with her role, she can't pull out."

"I'm not pulling out of my own accord," said Stella. "I can't stand staying in this old town! It's full of busybodies who are more excited about what Bob and I did than about their own affairs."

"Stella," the banker said in a reproving tone,

"you must not call the Selectmen busybodies. There are three of them, and they came to see me last night at my home," he went on, turning back to Peter. "They are responsible, intelligent family men."

"Nuts," said Stella.

Her father frowned. "They feel that if Stella and Bob Morehouse appear in a community project such as this play, after what happened the other night, they will seem to condone this example of juvenile delinquency. They have been trying to stop wild driving and reckless road games, and they pointed out to me that at least two teen-agers had been badly hurt while chicken racing."

Peter Howard threw up his hands in a gesture of defeat, and started away without speaking. This is the end, he was thinking. Not only Stella, who could be replaced if necessary, but Bob Morehouse, his leading man, was being snatched from the cast. He had spent considerable time coaching Bob and he had, he thought, succeeded in getting just the results he had hoped for. There wasn't the slightest use going on with the play at this point. With Bob out of the running, there wasn't any play, actually. Used as he was to setbacks in his profession, Peter was plunged into a despair deeper than any he had ever experienced.

For several minutes he stood in front of the barn, staring at the Reynolds' farmhouse across the road. He had a view of the side door of the house, and he was startled to hear the bang of the screen door as Farmer Reynolds hurtled past it and came running—really running, instead of ambling as usual—across the road.

"Mr. Howard! Mr. Howard! Banker Rand is wanted on the phone! There's been a train wreck at the crossing."

Stella's father was out of the car before the farmer had finished speaking. He strode across the yard toward the farmhouse.

"A wreck!" yelled Bob Morehouse, detaching himself from the group around Stella's car. "Hear that, Gil? A wreck! What're we doing here?" He was already in his own car and was turning it into the road before Gil caught up with it, leaping into the front seat beside his brother as Bob threw open the door without slowing down.

The rest of the crowd scattered toward their own cars. Stella motioned to Kate to get into her car, explaining, as she too drove across the yard:

"Dad's a stockholder in that railroad. He'll want to get down to the scene, but fast. We'll pick him up at the gate."

"All right, Stella; let's go." Banker Rand was grim-faced as he climbed into the front seat, crowding Kate without seeming to be aware of her presence. They joined what soon became a regular procession of cars, with all the boys and girls of the theatre group and Peter Howard in line. Bringing up the rear came Farmer Reynolds in his battered sedan with Hallie beside him, wiping her hands on the apron she had forgotten to take off.

Chapter 13

When they got to the scene of the train wreck, just outside Clyde's Gap, Kate was horrified at what she saw. The "crossing" was actually a bridge across Clyde's River, and the long train had evidently been derailed midway over the trestle. Five of the cars lay on one side and the other cars were canted at a perilous angle. The ambulances had apparently just arrived from nearby towns and the injured were being put on stretchers to be whisked away as soon as possible. Some police were already there, but the autos containing the theatre boys and girls had gotten through before the police cordon was established. There was no trouble about the Rand car; the cordon automatically opened for it, and Stella parked the car as close to the river as she dared.

"There's Bob down on the river bank!" Stella exclaimed as she braked to a stop. "What in the world is he doing? He's taking off his shoes. There he goes into the water!"

With a shock, Kate realized that some of the passengers must have been thrown clear of the wreck and had been pitched headlong into the river. Although the scene seemed to be in slow motion, Kate realized that it was hardly a second before Bob jumped into the river and was swimming with strong, firm strokes toward someone she could not see. She heard a car door slam and saw Stella running toward the spot where Bob Morehouse had taken off. Kate felt an almost personal pride as she watched Stella swim out after Bob.

Both Bob and Stella had won medals for their swimming prowess ever since they were ten years old. Kate herself was an indifferent swimmer but, she suddenly realized, there was much to be done near at hand. The fire truck from Clyde's Gap, equipped with a resuscitator, had just driven up, and there would be plenty for them to do.

Kate noticed an elderly man wandering around in an apparently aimless manner. He had a deep cut over one eye and tried ineffectually to dab away the blood. Mr. Rand had left the car at almost the same time that Stella did, and Kate could see him talking with an important-looking group of men.

She approached the old man quickly and put a detaining hand on his arm. "Why don't you sit down here on the grass for a minute?" she urged. "I'll get one of the interns to bandage your head."

"What happened?" the old man quivered. "Where are my glasses? I've lost my glasses."

"Kate, come over here, will you?" Gil shouted at her. "I think this woman has a broken arm. Could you loan us your bandanna?"

Kate made the old man comfortable and assured him that she would be back. Then she ran over to Gil and gave him the scarf he had asked for. In the meantime she had glimpsed a girl with a heavy brace on one foot, who was crying quietly and trembling, obviously too afraid to move. There were a number of scenes like these all about her. Kate was vaguely aware that all those engaged in the community show were busy doing what they could to help the distressed passengers. The firemen parked their truck close to the river's edge and set up an extension ladder which they clambered up and down. Those who had been trapped in the wreckage were carefully brought down to the ground, where two more ambulances had arrived from neighboring communities. It was a scene of ordered confusion, and it was remarkable how quickly the men worked. She had a glimpse of Bob Morehouse bringing a woman to the shore; close after him, Stella was swimming toward the same spot with what looked like a doll in one arm. Peter and Martina were wading offshore to help those who had managed to swim under their own power.

It was like a war scene, Kate decided, and yet in a way it seemed absolutely unreal, like a dream. There was very little sound from those who were badly injured, and even those who were helping spoke in low voices. She herself did not remember afterward speaking to those she tried to aid. The need was for action, rather than words.

"Mom, I find it hard to tell you what it was like," Kate told her mother later.

Evangeline Scott spoke soothingly to her daughter and insisted that she wash up and put on a pair of fresh slacks and a fresh blouse before she came to a light lunch. Kate was surprised to find when she looked in the bathroom mirror that her face was smudged with dirt and she had a slight cut under one eye. She could not recall how it had happened, although she had a vague impression that she had slipped on the mud near the shore and had fallen. It had not seemed important at the time, and she had gone on to help all she could without giving it another thought.

As she spooned up the soup her mother placed before her Kate felt calmer and gave her mother a more detailed account of what had happened near the wreck. Evangeline Scott listened without saying a word until Kate had finished. Then she looked fondly at her daughter and said:

"I understand that Stella Rand and Bob Morehouse covered themselves with glory in the rescue work they did. I hear from the postmaster that their picture will be in all the evening papers. But you haven't said anything about what you did. From the way you looked when you came in, you must have been fairly busy."

"I didn't do anything special," Kate protested. "There wasn't much I could do really."

"I marvel that you youngsters were able to do so much in the way of helping the victims of this disaster," Mrs. Scott continued. "It must have been a thoroughly shocking experience, even though you had no direct part in it."

"Most of us have had mock air raid alerts and have been taught some first aid at school," Kate explained. "Most important of all, I think, was what we were taught *not* to do. I can't answer for the others, of course, but subconsciously I must have remembered to keep out of the way of the firemen and the hospital attendants and to make myself useful without interfering. Things were pretty well under control when I left, and they were already starting to right the railroad cars and get them cleared off the track. As far as I could see, all of the badly injured had been taken away, and those who had only minor injuries were being treated on the spot."

"I am glad you were able to help so much," Mrs. Scott commented. "That nice Peter Howard phoned a few minutes before you came in and said that you would not have to be at the barn before tomorrow morning."

"Thank you, Mom," Kate said with a sinking feeling. In the excitement she had forgotten all about the play and about the fact that Stella Rand and Bob Morehouse were about to be withdrawn from the cast. Probably, she thought dismally, Peter was asking them to report to the barn the next day simply to tell them that they were all dismissed and that he was returning to New York. There was a dull ache in her heart as she looked ahead to an empty end of summer.

Even Stella Rand and Bob Morehouse were at the barn the next morning when they all gathered, waiting for the director to arrive.

"Those two are waiting to be kicked out officially," Gil said gloomily to Kate.

"They won't go alone," retorted Kate. "The play won't go on without them; we'll all be out of a job. I hear that this kind of thing often happens to regular actors, but we haven't the right to be called actors yet. Who's going to care, besides us, that our play flops before it's produced?"

"Peter Howard will," offered Gil.

"Oh, he'll get over it. He'll just take his play to New York and get it put on somewhere with a professional cast. This project of ours was only a tryout—a chance for Peter to find out if his play has a chance in a real theatre."

"Did you see this picture of Bob bringing in that half-drowned woman?" asked Gil, displaying a Boston newspaper which carried shots of various scenes at the train wreck site, with shots of both Bob and Stella Rand used lavishly to embellish the story. The train wreck had made headlines in all the big eastern papers, and several members of the cast had brought along copies which had arrived in town that morning. The enterprising photographer on the local paper had seized the opportunity to sell prints to out of town papers and news services.

"Gee, last night when I was trying to deliver my papers, I couldn't seem to get around fast enough to suit my customers," said Gil. "A lot of them were waiting outstide their front doors to grab the *Clyde Gap Clarion* before I could throw one on their porches."

Kate only half listened to Gil. She could see Peter Howard's car in the distance, and her spirits sank lower.

Now the axe will fall, she was thinking to herself. Nobody felt as badly about the collapse of the summer theatre project as she, Kate was sure. Gil wasn't really in the play; just an added attraction for the intermission. None of the others were even dreaming of a stage career, she knew. It was Kate Scott who was to be hurt the most. She had been looking forward to being "discovered" by some of the theatrical friends invited by Peter Howard to see the show.

I might have made an impression on some producer, she told herself, and Mom would have let me leave school and go to New York, in that case. I could have gotten some little job to pay my expenses at a professional school while waiting for a part in a play. But without any definite encouragement, without any proof that I have enough talent to warrant my leaving home, Mom would never consent to it."

Kate smiled wanly as Peter Howard came toward her, a broad grin on his face.

He looks as if he's glad to be rid of the whole project, she thought angrily. He doesn't even look sorry that he'll be leaving *me*."

Peter was waving enthusiastically to the others. "Gather round, kids!" he shouted. "I've got news for you."

"What kind of news?" Kate muttered.

"The best," boomed Peter. "Here, all of you! Into the barn with you. I don't hear any hammering to drown me out today, but that'll soon be remedied. And I tell you, my merry troupe, I'll be the happiest man alive to hear the old bang-bang again."

Kate and the others followed Peter into the barn without much enthusiasm. It was hard to work up any feeling of eagerness when you were to be told that your services were no longer required.

"I wonder if we have to give the money back to Banker Rand," Gil said to Kate in a low tone.

"I don't know. I should think so."

"Dad wouldn't think of taking any of the money back," Stella said in a fierce whisper.

There was a loud "sh" from the other members of the cast and the crew, and Peter, jumping up on the newly built stage, held up both hands for silence.

"The reason I'm late," he began, "is because

I went to a meeting called by the Board of Selectmen this morning in the Town Hall. I went there by request, I might add," he said as he noted the gloomy faces that surrounded him. "I didn't know what the meeting was all about, so I didn't call even Miss Dawson to tell her that I was going."

There was a dead silence as Peter paused, and he said with some spirit:

"I have rarely seen such a cold audience. I was going to lead up to my finale gradually, but I can see I had better begin at the finale and go backward. So I'll say right off—everything's going to be all right. Stella and Bob Morehouse will continue to be in the cast, and our show will be put on just as we had planned. But there is one condition."

After a minute of dazed silence there was a brief spattering of applause. Gil even went so far as to utter a weak "hurray." Martina Dawson spoke up and said in a crisp voice:

"Perhaps you'd better tell us quickly what that one condition is. If it's something we can't possibly do—"

"No, the condition is a very simple one," Peter

said with a smile. "I am only to repeat to you what was said at that meeting and I want you all to listen very carefully, because the Selectmen of Clyde's Gap are a fine group of men. They feel that if you, as members of the high school, can know and understand the problems presented by juvenile delinquency, you will have the makings of a splendid lot of citizens.

"First of all, I think you all began to realize yesterday, when that train wreck occurred, that there is nothing thrilling about being maimed or injured for life. Any one of you may be in a disastrous accident at any time. We live in that kind of world. If you go out looking for trouble, you have nine chances out of ten to find it right here in Clyde's Gap."

Peter paused and took a long breath. Then, speaking slowly and with emphasis, he went on, "What the selectmen actually said was something like this:

"The future rests in your hands. Each of you listening to me this morning has the choice of becoming an asset to the community or a liability. If you choose to become an asset, every person will try to help you. The town of Clyde's

Gap, and in fact the people of every city, large and small, will do their best to make your life happy and successful. This is not a matter of sentiment alone; it is also a matter of dollars and cents. The cost of juvenile delinquency runs into many millions of dollars. The cost in lives lost and in near-fatal injuries will perhaps never be known precisely. I have often heard the youngsters of your generation saying that your parents and older folks in general do not understand you and won't help you. I assure you they do understand."

A murmur ran through the crowd as he stopped speaking. Martina Dawson raised her hand for quiet.

"Now, boys and girls," she told them, "Peter Howard has fulfilled the condition. He has repeated to you what the Selectmen said, and you have listened carefully. But I think you should do more. I think you should make the kind of response that will show these fine men that you appreciate the faith in you they have shown in letting the show go on with Stella Rand and Bob Morehouse in the cast. I think you should promise, here in public, that as far as you representative young people of Clyde's Gap are concerned, there will be no more chicken racing, no careless driving, no senseless brawls between you and the young men and women of other towns, as have occurred in so many communities. Mr. Howard, will you ask for a show of hands from those who make this solemn promise?"

"Gladly," said Peter. "All right, my young friends. All in favor of Miss Dawson's promise raise their right hands."

Every right hand in the barn shot up, some of them waving frantically in the effort to be convincing.

"Very well," said Peter. "It's official. Let's give ourselves a great big round of applause."

There was a burst of hand-clapping and stomping that threatened the new reinforcements of the barn's foundations.

"One more detail," said Peter. "The Selectmen took a vote of their own. They voted a citation—something elaborately framed and glass-covered, to be hung in the City Hall. It will state that Miss Stella Rand and Mr. Robert Morehouse are hereby given an award of honor for their magnificent actions, without regard to their own safety, in rescuing victims of the train wreck. They were not only the first to bring certain victims to shore when, due to their injuries and shocks, they were in grave danger of drowning, but they continued to save many others who had been thrown into the water.

"That the Selectmen would also vote to rescind their former demand that these two members of the cast of our play be withdrawn," Peter went on, "was a foregone conclusion. And now, may I add to the honors that have been bestowed upon these two members of our group my own congratulations?"

Peter moved toward Stella Rand, who was looking stunned, and seized her hand. "Good girl," he said. Then, turning to Bob, he caught him by the other hand. "Great guy," he pronounced solemnly. "What do you say, Gang?"

No words were distinguishable in what the gang shouted, but the approval of the crowd was unmistakable. When the uproar died down after a clamorous yell for "Speech, Bob! Speech!" Bob did speak.

"Aw," he said.

Chapter 14

There was increasing tension in the air the week before the show was to go on. Kate marveled at how smooth they had all become in the delivery of their lines and at how she herself stepped into her role, time after time, without even needing to glance at the script.

The barn, too, in some way was miraculously transformed. One day it was just a crude attempt to emulate a professional summer theatre; the next day the flats went up, the furniture was moved into place and the folding camp chairs arranged in front of the stage. Even the curtains which her mother had made swung with professional precision from either side and effectively made the stage world a thing apart from the audience. To Kate's bedazzled eyes the project which she had dreamed of was suddenly full-blown and far exceeded her expectations.

For some reason, Gil Morehouse had not rehearsed at any time in front of the company.

Peter had insisted that he coach him alone, and as a consequence Kate had no idea what arias he was going to sing or how they would be presented. But by this time she trusted Peter Howard's direction implicitly.

Kate had had little chance to talk with Peter alone lately, and he had sought no further dates. But somehow that did not make any difference. She saw him every day, and that was enough. It was true he still urged her to think of something sad before she came on in the second act. At one time he suggested that she remember their frightening experience in the mine. But that had been a mistake; within just a few days the experience in the mine had assumed the proportions of a romantic interlude and she could fall asleep at night dreaming of that moment when she had kept talking to bolster Peter's spirits. It was an indication, she was sure, of how much he really needed her, despite his sophistication.

Yet in spite of the fact that the tickets had been selling so well that even Peter could find no fault with the publicity, the members of the cast were increasingly uneasy. The director kept rehearsing them over and over again, scolding them whenever they got careless and changed a line or stuttered over a word. Kate began to wonder if Peter had lost confidence in them and if, after all, he was going sooner or later to leave them to their own resources.

Then one night, as they finished rehearsing, Peter called them all together. There was an electric quality in the air that Kate could feel. She was not disappointed when Peter made his announcement—something important was about to happen.

"I have been talking with the costume committee chairman," he began quietly, "and she tells me that everything is now ready. The property committee has had its work completed for several days, as you well know, and even the ticket booth, although it still needs a coat of paint, is all set up. So—"

Peter paused for effect in a heavy silence. No one seemed to be breathing. Peter smiled to show he was not teasing and went on:

"Tomorrow will be Thursday and, as you know, the show opens Saturday night. Therefore I am going to call a full dress rehearsal for tomorrow night at eight. You will be in your dressing rooms, please, at six o'clock, and you will report to me on stage no later than seven-thirty. You must be in costume, your make-up must be complete, and of course you must know your lines as if you had been born with them in your minds.

"The stage crew must be ready to handle the lighting and to pull and draw the curtains just as they will do on Saturday night. I will not interrupt the play at any time, no matter how many boners you pull. You will assume that the audience is in place and that you have to talk above the rustling of the programs and the occasional coughing that every actor has to contend with. Remember not to mumble but to speak clearly and to project your voices so that they can be heard in the last row."

"What about Gil Morehouse?" Kate inquired.

"He'll be here," Peter promised. "And he will appear during the intermission as I told you he would. But remember, when he goes into his act, you are not to forget that you are here not to be entertained but to work. If I hear any applause or any noise whatsoever in the wings, I will personally see to it that you rehearse twenty times

on Friday." With a brilliant smile Peter concluded, "That's all, Gang. Get as much rest as
you can tomorrow and report here at six o'clock
sharp. Remember I am counting on you to do me
proud."

Kate felt the sting of tears behind her eyes as
she turned docilely and walked out with the rest
of the crowd.

Thursday night promptly at six everyone appeared on the stage. When Peter saw them he
scowled. Apparently the cast had been unable to
wait until the hour he set and had been there in
plenty of time to get dressed before their director appeared. It was evident they expected to be
praised for their eagerness. But Peter Howard,
as they were to discover, was anything but
pleased.

"You're going to be all tired out by eight
o'clock," he said crossly. "I told you to report at
six, and that's what I meant. Now I want all of
you to go back to your dressing rooms and remove all your make-up. Be sure you don't get it
on your dresses or on the collars of your shirts.
Then I will take you one at a time and work with

the make-up man to see that you each look fairly human and not like clowns. I want the girls to remember, when they sit down, to lift their skirts. Otherwise you'll be running around the stage in crumpled dresses."

For the next hour things proceeded in an orderly and subdued fashion. Peter wholeheartedly approved of Kate's costume, which her mother had made of white voile with inserts of imitation Irish lace. He vetoed the sash, however, and suggested instead that a piece of the red satin be used for a flat bow on top of her pale gold hair.

Stella's dress was of green cotton with puffed sleeves and a square neck. Kate thought it vastly becoming—far more so than the shorts and pullovers the Stella ordinarily wore. Bob Morehouse's costume was a ragged shirt and a pair of overalls, while Jim Reynolds wore the usual work clothes that he was accustomed to don around his own farm.

But it remained for Martina Dawson to put them all in the shade. Her floor-length "travelling costume" had a bell-shaped skirt. She wore a shirtwaist with a high boned collar and numerous lace insertions. The jacket was outlined in black soutache braid and was a shade of blue that exactly matched her eyes. Although Kate knew she was wearing a wig, the dark brown pompadour in which the hair was arranged was so becoming that again Kate felt, as she had in Stella's case, that Miss Dawson should have been born in an earlier era.

Peter allowed them to have a glass of milk or of fruit juice, which he supplied from cartons in his own car, before he actually called for the rehearsal to begin. Then, with a measured tread, he walked off the stage and out into the last row of seats. In order to make the scene realistic he began coughing and mumbling to himself until the cast actually felt that it was opening night. All at once he barked:

"Okay, Gang. Lights, curtain, action!"

Kate, alone on the stage, was surprised at how calm she felt. She saw now the wisdom of Peter's constant rehearsals, boring as they had often seemed. She knew that she could not forget her lines and probably would never forget them. She prepared to dance across the stage toward the door through which Stella, Bob and Henry would enter. The boy who was to open the curtain was already standing in the wings, his hands on the rope of the pulley. He was white-faced and tense, and as he pulled on the rope it happened: the curtain stuck.

True to his promise, Peter did not offer any advice but instead began to cough again and stomp his feet. Kate felt sorry for the boy who was pulling so frantically on the rope. Then she saw that Gil Morehouse was coming to the rescue, and a second later the curtain swung smoothly back and Kate went into the first scene.

The four of them were caught up in the parts they were playing, and the player piano—now electrically operated from the wings—began to play, "Oh, You Beautiful Doll." As they danced around the stage Kate felt that her heart would burst with happiness. This was indeed a supreme moment; the play was on its way to success.

Then, as the piano continued to play and they continued to dance, Kate began to get panicky. They were supposed to take only a few turns before Farmer Reynolds entered.

Stage directions called for the irate farmer to stride over toward the piano and make a gesture, at which the music would cease. But time went on and Farmer Reynolds did not appear. Once more Peter began to cough loudly from his seat in the rear. Then, almost as the last note on the piano was played, Jim Reynolds did come barging through the door. He forgot to go over to the piano but instead said loudly:

"Them durned chickens got out again; had to chase 'em back before I could come over here."

The boy who was operating the player piano had the wit to stop the mechanism. Jim Reynolds stood in the middle of the floor. Bob Morehouse quickly came in with his line and the farmer seemed to realize all at once that he was on the stage. Kate, Stella and Henry made their exit in a most realistic fashion. Kate had never in her life been so thankful as to be away from the footlights. Surely the worst was now over!

She looked at Martina Dawson, seemingly so quiet and composed, as she waited before the young man who was playing the part of her theatrical agent. Kate resolutely tore her eyes away and concentrated on the fact that she must go back on the stage the moment Jim Reynolds made his exit. She was ready and waiting when she saw the farmer come out, and she tiptoed back onto the stage according to the directions she was supposed to follow. During the brief love scene that was to follow the boy controlling the lights was supposed to dim them gradually, indicating that twilight was falling.

He took his job seriously, Kate thought with some bitterness, as the lights grew dimmer and dimmer until finally they went out altogether with the suddenness of a tropic nightfall. Bob struck a match to light the old-fashioned lamp as he was supposed to do, but before he could take off the chimney the lights came on again with the full force of midday. Kate and Bob, ignoring this mishap, doggedly went on with their lines, but again Kate was grateful when she could make a retreat to the safe haven of the dressing room. There she sank onto the bench before the improvised table and held her head in her hands.

"What will Peter think of us?" she wailed to Stella. "We are certainly acting like a bunch of rank amateurs—and I do mean rank."

"Well, we are amateurs," Stella said reasonably. "You can't count a junior play as red-hot experience."

"But this is Peter's own play," Kate pointed

out, "and there will be friends of his from New York out there in the first night audience. Wait till I get hold of that Morton—he just ruined my big scene with Bob!"

But eventually the curtains were drawn at the close of the first act and Gil Morehouse, looking entirely unlike himself in tight black slacks and a white silk shirt, went out before the curtains. The next moment his hearty young baritone rang through the almost empty barn. Kate and the others, ignoring Peter's instructions, crowded into the wings to peep at the performer, who was singing without benefit of accompaniment.

Kate was astonished at the change professional coaching had made in Gil's presentation. His every movement now had a polish that would have done credit to a veteran performer. He had not changed his routine conspicuously, but when he started to swing the melody the little solo dance he had always done became less conspicuous. His movements were smooth, almost nonchalant, but even to Kate they had a professional air.

"Wowie!" Henry Johnson said, hardly daring to breathe. "I didn't think old Gil had it in him.

He's got bounce!"

When Act Two began Kate did not think that anything more could go wrong. By this time the boy operating the curtains was working with sure precision and the one who was manipulating the lights had evidently learned his lesson. He managed to give a very creditable imitation of summer dawn flooding the countryside, at the same time turning on the mechanical bird and blowing bird whistles. He varied this by occasionally mooing like a cow and neighing like a horse.

"Talk about a one-man band," Henry whispered to Kate, as she waited to make her entrance. "That guy wouldn't have anything on our pal Morton."

Kate made her entrance on cue, feeling like an experienced actress. To her intense astonishment, she suddenly found herself face down on the floor. She had forgotten that the hooked rug borrowed from her mother's attic was badly torn in one spot. She tripped over it and for a second after she struck the floor could not get her wind. But Bob proved equal to the occasion.

"I've been meaning to tell Paw that he oughta get that rug fixed," Bob ad-libbed. "You hurt?"

he inquired, as he helped her to her feet.

"No, just shook up," Kate said, entering into the spirit of the fiasco. Then she went into her lines. But, try as she would, she could not get the proper sadness into her voice and attitude, even after Martina, as the glamorous movie star, had made her entrance onto the stage. She was not acting as if she had just lost the boy she loved, Kate realized. Rather, she felt she had just been presented with the world on a silver platter. She made her exit for the last time and stood watching the final scenes of the play.

This time Jim Reynolds was backstage, ready to go on, a full ten minutes before his cue. Kate nodded and smiled at him approvingly. But impressed with his own importantce, as the actor who had the final line in the play, he gave Kate only the briefest nod. Then, all at once, Martina Dawson was standing beside her, her eyes sparkling with the knowledge that she had played her part well. Farmer Reynolds slouched onto the stage with an empty milk pail in either hand. He looked reproachfully at Bob Morehouse, who was wearing his Sunday suit in order to impress the movie star. Curtly, he ordered his "son" to get into overalls and help with the morning chores.

As if the sound of his voice had been a signal, there was a sudden clucking from the open door of the barn. Kate craned her neck in bewilderment. And then she saw them; the white leghorns that were the farmer's pride and joy had followed their owner across the road and were now busily pecking their way down the center aisle, looking for seeds in the cracks of the floor. Kate could not stand it; she burst into tears.

It was almost an hour later that Kate, having removed her costume and makeup, had the courage to venture out of the dressing room. Peter had been surprisingly indulgent about the various accidents that had befallen them and reminded them of the old adage: that a poor dress rehearsal meant a fine opening performance. Nevertheless Kate was thoroughly downcast. In her mind every action of the cast was a reflection on her own poor management. She was stealing past one of the flats backstage when she heard what sounded very much like someone crying. Then, a moment later, Peter's voice was unmistakably raised in a muffled shout of laughter.

"In case you don't know it, Tina," he said in a choked voice, "you saw a mighty fine piece of acting tonight by yours truly. I had to keep a straight face while I was lecturing the kids when all I wanted to do was lie down on the floor and howl. I thought I had written a tragedy, but it turns out I wrote the funniest comedy of the year."

"Never mind." Martina Dawson sounded very soothing. "New York was never like this, and I am sure it never will be. You need not be afraid of a repeat performance."

Peter's voice, husky and serious, answered her: "I'll never be afraid of a repeat performance as long as you are right there beside me, my darling!"

"Oh, Peter!"

"I know I promised you a honeymoon trip to Bermuda, but I guess you'll have to settle for one in New York. I just heard my play is to be produced off-Broadway this fall. How will you like being the wife of a successful playwright?"

The last sound Kate heard as she tiptoed quietly to the door was Martina Dawson's smug: "M-m-m-m. . . ."

Chapter 15

When the big night finally arrived, Kate found herself peering through the curtains with a singular lack of interest. Ever since she had discovered that she had completely misunderstood Peter Howard's kindness toward her, Kate had felt terribly depressed. She was glad that no one had seen her mortification on Thursday night when she had found out that Martina and Peter were planning on a future together. Everyone was so busy, moreover, that no one noticed her apathy. Only Stella, standing beside her now, had a glimmering of her friend's state of mind.

"Ooh, look at the first row," Stella said. "I hear Peter Howard reserved the whole front row for his theatrical friends. They don't look like actors or actresses to me," Stella continued.

"What do you think, Kate?"

"I don't know," Kate said languidly. "I guess maybe they're more directors or producers than they are actors. Maybe the women with them are their wives."

Stella took her eye from the crack in the curtain and turned to stare at her friend. "What's the matter with you, Kate? You were the one who started this whole thing, and now you act as if you couldn't wait for it to be over."

Kate mentally shook herself. It would never do to let Stella know she was suffering from a broken heart. "I'm all right," she protested; "just a little tired and let down after all the excitement of these past weeks. I meant to tell you, Stella," she added, hastily changing the subject, "how pretty you look in your costume. It seemed to me I saw Bob Morehouse looking at you with great admiration."

"I'd rather it was Henry Johnson," Stella said unexpectedly. "I've kind of lost interest in Bob."

Kate sensed rather than saw that Peter had come up behind them. Stella diplomatically went back to the dressing room and Kate, furious with herself as she felt her color rising, started to follow her. Her heart ached so as she looked at Peter she thought he must surely know how she felt. His light beige suit was not exactly a tuxedo, but with the pleated bosom of his silk shirt showing and a black bow tie, the effect was quite formal. He grinned at her impersonally and nodded toward the first row:

"See that guy in the plaid sports jacket and red shirt? He's one of the big New York agents," Peter said. "And that stout man next to him, who looks something like Stella's father, is the producer who will put on my play this fall. So I want you to act for all you're worth, Kate, and remember what I told you about looking sad in Act Two."

"I'll look sad," Kate promised dully. She thought how easy it was going to be to follow his instructions now.

"Good. That is just the tone I want." Peter looked at her keenly, then gave her a quick hug. "I almost forgot; Tina wants you to stop by her 'dressing room' before you go on tonight. Good luck, Kate; I'm counting on you more than anyone else."

Kate went toward the crude dressing room that

had been built in back of the barn. A curtain stretched down the middle of it, and Kate and Stella shared one side while Martina Dawson, as the star, had the other side. Stella was apparently engaged in some business of her own and was not in the room, but the minute Kate said tentatively: "Miss Dawson?" the teacher responded warmly with an invitation to come to her side of the curtain.

Martina was busy drawing lines on her face to simulate an appearance of age. She did not stop but motioned Kate to the one empty chair near the dressing table and continued to apply her make-up.

"How are you feeling—about tonight's performance, I mean?" Martina inquired.

"All right," Kate said indifferently.

"It's always quite a letdown when you reach the final point where all that you've dreamed of comes true," Martina said wisely. She stole a glance at Kate and went on applying her make-up. "But don't let it get you down, my dear. You have a long, full life ahead of you. By this time next year tonight will be just a memory— a pleasant one, I hope."

"Peter said there are a producer and an agent in the audience," Kate said after a few seconds. "He pointed them out to me."

Martina completed her make-up and swung around so that she was facing Kate. Her expression was serious, and she stretched out her hand as if to lay it on Kate's knee. But apparently she thought better of it and contented herself with saying earnestly:

"Kate, I don't want you to get your hopes up. You are still very young, and there is plenty of time for you to get theatrical training and to make a career of the theatre, if that is what you want. I know that from a distance the world of the theatre seems glamorous and easy to attain. But believe me, Peter has had to work very hard ever since he was graduated, and he has fought for the recognition he now has. It is one of the most difficult professions, although it is extremely rewarding."

Kate looked at her teacher pityingly. Miss Dawson was trying to discourage her, so that she would not continue to follow her plan to go to New York. Kate was confident that Peter would help her if she told him how much she wanted a theatrical career.

"Thank you for your advice," Kate said primly, as she stood up, "but it is close to curtain time, Miss Dawson, and I am the first one on the stage, you know."

"Yes, I know," Martina smiled, "and I congratulate you on a job well done."

"You're good, too," Kate murmured grudgingly. "But now I really must fly."

"Just one second more," Martina begged, as she fumbled at the buttons of her old-fashioned shirtwaist. "I have a feeling, Kate that you know what I am about to tell you. However, I don't know how you found out, because Peter and I thought we kept our secret very well."

"I know you are planning to get married," Kate admitted. "I overheard you the night of the dress rehearsal. Could I be the flower girl?" she asked impudently.

Martina looked at her gravely. Then, while Kate stared, she pulled out a silver chain from around her neck. On it were strung a sparkling diamond engagement ring and a wide platinum band.

"We are already married, Kate," Martina said

softly, and in spite of the make-up her face looked young and vulnerable. "We slipped away ten days ago, and we were going to announce our marriage right after the show closed. I am glad now that you are the first to know."

Kate's eyes fastened on the twinkling diamond as if she were hypnotized. Then, with a choked sob, she ran to the other side of the curtain and buried her head in her arms.

"Say, what gives?" Stella demanded, rushing in at the last minute. "You look as if you'd lost your last friend."

"I'm practising for the second act," Kate said, pulling herself together. "Peter says I don't look sad enough in the opening scene of Act Two when I find out I've lost the man I love."

Stella looked at her shrewdly. "But this is Act One, remember? You're supposed to make with the smiles and the gay laughter. Better hurry; it's only five minutes to curtain time."

Afterward Kate thought that if the audience had really known her innermost feelings they would have given her great credit for her acting in the opening scene of the play. Actually she was so used to rehearsing the part that she fell naturally into the role of the light-hearted school-girl and danced around with Bob Morehouse to the strains of "Oh, You Beautiful Doll" as if she didn't have a care in the world.

Still, Kate was surprised when, following Jim Reynolds' entrance, the audience broke into spontaneous applause. Somehow she had not realized while rehearsing to many rows of empty chairs, that tonight they would be filled with people who would understand and applaud. Suddenly every other thought vanished from her mind, and she really was the character she was supposed to portray. The audience seemed to reach out to her, enjoying her in a world of make-believe. From then on she thought only of the play and of the story it was telling.

As they had been instructed to do, all members of the cast stayed away from the curtains during Gil's intermission performance. Kate knew, from the tremendous applause and the demand for encores, that Gil was scoring a great success. But she did not let her thoughts dwell on it. Instead she concentrated on giving her role in the opening scene of Act Two the best interpretation she could possibly manage.

"Sort of a wedding present to Peter," she told herself with a wry smile.

It was like coming back to a familiar spot when the play ended and she and all the others were called out to take their bows. There was a lovely old-fashioned bouquet from her mother and a great sheaf of pink roses from Peter. Stella had a basket of flowers from her father which was so huge she could easily have hidden behind it. Martina Dawson took her bows alone and carried only a small bouquet of red roses, which Kate was sure had been sent by Peter. The teacher was surrounded by ostentatious floral offerings and Kate suspected that many of Peter's friends had already heard the news of his recent marriage.

Since the dressing rooms were small and inadequate, the members of the cast stayed on stage behind the closed curtains and Peter brought his important theatrical friends back to meet them individually. Kate accepted their praise numbly and assured them that she would be at the small supper party Peter had planned at the Berkshire Chalet.

Finally only members of the cast were left on

stage when Peter brought in the men he had pointed out to Kate before the show started. The producer—the one who looked like Stella's father—was quiet and reserved. But the agent was almost trembling with excitement. His dark eyes snapped and he kept running his fingers through his wavy hair.

"Pete Howard," he said as he pumped Gil's hand, "you've done it again. How you ever found this guy in such a God-forsaken corner of the woods is beyond me. Frankly, I didn't believe your wire. But now that I've caught the act, I don't mind telling you that you have a real piece of property here. Yes sir, a real piece of property."

"You make him sound like a horse," Henry Johnson clowned, and Stella giggled. But there were no answering smiles on the faces of the agent and the producer. Instead they were looking at Gil Morehouse as if they had suddenly found a gold nugget at the bottom of a stream. They glanced briefly at each other and then nodded to Peter.

"Gil, I have some pretty special news for you," Peter said, clearing his throat. "These two men feel that you have a tremendous amount of talent. They are willing to back you and see that you get the proper training and help you launch a career. It would mean that you would have to come to New York, but not that you would have to give up school. You could hire a tutor and complete your high school education. What do you say?"

Gil was shaking his head negatively. "I can't leave Clyde's Gap," he said firmly.

This pronouncement seemed to stun the producer and agent. It was the latter who found his voice first.

"You can't use a million dollars?" he demanded. "Oh, come off it, kid. You can't be completely nuts."

"Wait'll you hear that one of your platters has sold a hundred thousand copies," the producer put in. "And that is just the beginning, boy. By the time you get through with your training you'll be on your way. Me and Al here know how to put a talent across."

Gil continued to stand silent, a stubborn look on his face. Kate, who had rather expected that she would be offered a chance to train for the stage, could not quite comprehend what was going on. Evidently all her efforts, although the best she could make, were not good enough. On the other hand, Gil, who had made no effort at all, was being offered a golden opportunity.

Again Gil shook his head. "It's aw'fly nice of you," he began, and the producer looked as if he were about to explode, "but I am needed here!"

"But, Gil," Kate said earnestly, "you can't turn down this offer just like that. At least tell these men that you will think it over."

Gil turned to her with a look of surprise. "You mean you want me to go?" he asked.

"Of course you must go." For some reason Kate felt that she and Gil were alone. The others had faded to insignificance.

"Then who will look after you?" Gil demanded. "You get carried away by a new idea, Kate, and when it doesn't pan out as you expected you get terribly hurt. I sort of figured to be around when you needed a shoulder to bawl on."

"Oh, Gil, don't be a goon," Kate said impatiently. "You're not going to the North Pole or the moon. We'll be in touch all the time. I'll even persuade Mom to take me down to New York for the Labor Day weekend."

"Is that a promise, Kate?"

When she nodded, Gil grinned and held out his hand to the agent. "It's a deal," he said as they shook hands. "I'll never figure out why you picked on me. Anyway, I'll give it all I've got. Say, I'm starved. Did I hear something about supper at the Berkshire Chalet?"

Gil brought Kate home after supper, and they sat silently in the scented dark for long minutes.

"I hate for this 'first night' to be over," said Kate finally, breaking into the insect chorus that swelled around them.

"Me, too," said Gil. "It's a sort of the beginning of the end, isn't it?"

"No," said Kate, "it's only the end of the beginning. We've grown up, lover boy."

"Don't say a thing like that unless you mean it, Kate."

"It's just a slang expression, Gil."

"I know. But when we're together like this slang seems—well, uncouth. I'm trying to tell you that what I feel for you is real love, Kate darling."

"Love." Kate sat quietly without speaking

after she had repeated the word softly. "I suppose you know that I made a mistake this summer. I thought I was in love with somebody, but I've found out that there is no such thing as one-sided love. The other—the man—wasn't in love with me; never even thought of me in that way. When I discovered that, I realized that what I had felt wasn't love at all."

"It was infatuation," said Gil soberly.

"Yes, I guess you could call it that," agreed Kate. "What I'm trying to tell you, Gil, is that when you say you love me, you are being very flattering, and I appreciate it. But I'm afraid of the word 'love' now, and I think we'd better not speak of love till we both—"

"That's okay by me," said Gil huskily, "just so you remember that I—just so, when I go to New York, you don't forget me."

"I could never forget you, Gil," said Kate.

She kissed him solemnly for a long minute, then slid out of the car.